AF394630

For my dad, who loved all manner of gangster movies.

STREET WALKIN' MAN

by Constantine Furman

STREET WALKIN' MAN
Second Edition

ISBN-13: 978-1-7344730-3-2
ISBN-10: 1727225007

This is a work of fiction. All the characters and events portrayed in this book are either products of the author's imagination or are used fictitiously.

Cover photography by Matt Payne, www.mattpaynemedia.com
John Fetaccini portrayed by Constantine Furman.
Cora Secillia portrayed by Heather Lerch.
Special thanks to Melissa Dock.

TABLE OF CONTENTS

CHAPTER ONE - Street Walkin' Couple

In the middle of Ohio was the city of Klaude. It was fairly large as far as cities in Ohio go, about the size of Seattle or New Orleans, but nowhere near competitive with the coastal big-boys of Los Angeles or New York.

Within Klaude, the city was divided up into four sections: the northwest corner where the middle-class lived, the northeast section where the rich people lived, downtown where city hall and the police stations were in the center section of the city, and the southwest racially-diverse corner was known as Proton. Then there was Puptown, the southern part of the city where the poorer people lived. Many Italians and Irish but others of the Caucasian persuasion as well.

It was on a wet, dreary street one night in Puptown in 2014 where a priest was working overtime. "Jerry's Kids?" he asked to passersby. "Help Jerry's Kids?" The clip-clopping of the passing footsteps on concrete gave the impression of horses in a parade.

Every so often, someone would toss some money or some change into his little black kettle that glistened in the street lights. But something wasn't quite right; this priest was far too young to be working so late for charity. Not to mention, his voice was far too raspy to be trusted as a voice of the church. It sounded somewhat like older Al Pacino and didn't match his younger age. But apparently, those walking by were none the wiser as they kept forking over their money.

"Please help these unfortunate youngsters," the priest entreated. "Give to Jerry's Kids if you can, please."

The pleading worked. More and more money went into the pot. As the walkers thinned out and eventually disappeared entirely, the priest clocked the area. With no one in the immediate vicinity paying him any mind, he picked up his little shiny kettle and headed off.

In a nearby alley, the slight drizzle was being shielded by awnings and other building paraphernalia jutting out above. A large, dingy green dumpster sitting nearby had one of the lids overturned backwards. The priest made his way into the alley, holding the kettle close to his chest. As he closed in on the dumpster, some rustling could be heard nearby. The priest paid it no mind as it sounded like trash in the wind.

"Ease away from the cash, Father," an ominous voice called out.

The priest stopped in his tracks. He placed the kettle onto the alley floor and turned back to find two young punks, hardly out of high school—if that—staring him down, glinting switchblades at the ready.

"But this is all I've got," the priest explained.

"Give us the money, NOW!" the scarier of the two commanded.

The priest began to look around as if trying to find some hidden passageway out. As he slowly backed away, his back hit the dumpster, causing the resultant metallic clang to reverberate throughout the alley. Meanwhile, the punks had advanced on the kettle and already had it in their grasp.

The taller of the two grabbed a dollar bill and tossed it at the priest's wet feet. "Something for the collection plate, Father," he chortled.

Laughing, the dickish duo started to run off, their footfalls clomping on the wet concrete. A loud whistle brought them to a sudden stop. *"The hell?"* they both thought as they looked to one another.

The two punks slowly turned around only for a somewhat quiet gunshot to blow the taller kid's switchblade clean out of his hands. He didn't even know it'd been knocked away until it flew out of his hands.

"Fuck!" the taller kid shouted as he fanned his hands in pain.

The wilder punk looked back and couldn't believe the priest had a .38 Special trained on him. The gunshots were much quieter than normal thanks to a special lighter pressure load in the bullets made specifically to attract as little attention as possible.

"You're next, baby," the priest said as coolly as his gravelly voice would permit.

"Man, screw this!" the wilder punk yelled as he dropped the kettle to the ground and he and his taller counterpart beat cheeks out of there.

The priest slightly smiled, then made the sign of the cross admonishing to the duo, "Go with God."

Looking around and finding himself alone at last, the priest pulled his collar and smock away, revealing a deep red sweater and black slacks a size or so too big underneath. He tossed the priest's getup into the dumpster, then proceeded to pull out a brown snap-brim fedora and a wool, ankle-length, black overcoat. They were immediately thrown on, completely eradicating the priest that stood there moments ago.

Standing in the absent padre's place was John Fetaccini, street walkin' man. At 34, the half-Irish, half-Italian hood seemed far more at home in the alley than the priest of before did. He resembled Marlon Brando's incarnation of Don Corleone as a young man, though without the moustache. He had a wide, moon face with thick, black hair, paw-like hands with prominent knuckles, and used his straight-hanging overcoat to hide the overweightness brought about by a lifetime of junk food and sodas.

This John Fetaccini fellow scooped the wet money into his coat's deep pockets. "*They should be good to go by the time I get home*," he thought, perhaps trying to fool himself. He dropped the kettle to the ground, leaving it behind as it echoed across the pavement.

The streets of downtown Klaude were littered with newspapers and other trash that the windy breezes seemed to enjoy tossing about like children's streamers.

John fidgeted in his pockets as he moved between two large buildings. Police sirens suddenly pierced the air, offending his ears, and causing him to involuntarily duck in beneath his coat collar and hat brim like a scared turtle. For good measure, he stepped into a corner shadow waiting in darkness as a duo of police cars screamed down the street. The hood's nose and right eye inched out from the shadow. Confident the coast was clear, he moved on.

As John rounded a street corner, gunshots rang out in the distance. John's face barely registered indifference towards them. A group of suspicious-looking street urchins passed him going the other way. "Hey John!" and "Yo, John"s rang out from them. He smiled and slightly waved as they parted ways. Nearby, John spotted a couple of lurid-looking streetwalkers. Both of them waved flirtatiously at him. As if out of courtesy, he waved back.

"Hey cowboy," the platinum blonde cooed. "Wanna have some fun?"

John smiled to himself, momentarily entertaining the thought, but then espoused, "I'll pass on the crotch tartar, thanks."

The blonde's mouth dropped in a combination of shock and offense. Her taller redhead friend chuckled as she admitted, "Dude's got your number, Linda."

The blonde cut her eyes at the redhead. "Shut up," she growled. "And don't call me that,"

"Oh honey..." the redhead calmly waved her off.

At Klaude Stadium—the city's premiere sports arena, hosting everything from basketball games to, even once, a three-hour Bruce Springsteen concert that threatened to destroy its crude construction—the excitement from within could be heard from outside. A large, garish sign was splayed for all to see announcing a title match for a Mixed Martial Arts fight between one Stoney Abbler and Randy Rimms.

John Fetaccini slowly ambled into the parking lot. Looking over the cars, he wondered to himself if he would ever own one to tool around town in. But if he didn't, at least he got plenty of exercise on foot. As he closed in on the arena, he made visible a plastic pass hanging around his neck allowing entrance from the guards on hand.

MMA fans roared their approval as two fighters, one Hispanic, the other black, slugged and kicked it out for domination of the center of the ring. The blows the two fighters landed sent sweat and blood flying into the front rows like the splatter of a Gallagher show.

The stench of the place was an overpowering mix of popcorn, stale hot dogs, and cheap beer. John made his way past some cheering fight fans to find his empty seat.

"Kick his ass!" one fan shouted.

"Knock him into next week!" another demanded.

John plopped down in his seat, seemingly disinterested in the fight and happy to be off his feet finally.

The MMA champs blasted away at each other in a flurry of blows that would've taken down any normal man. The bell rang, but its tinny end of the round didn't register and the two fighters continued punching each other. Or maybe they heard it and didn't care. Either way, the rather diminutive referee jumped between the two and succeeded in pushing them apart. The bell rang several more times in a desperate attempt to get the fighters to settle down.

John's attention was suddenly piqued. Not by the fighters, but by the ring card girl climbing into the ring.

She looked to be in her late twenties, with a jaw-line length, ink-black bob hairstyle. She had a heart-shaped face with a high, curved forehead. She wore a turquoise-colored, one-piece swimsuit-style outfit that left little—if anything—to the imagination.

Seeing as the fighters had finally returned to their corners, insults and bad blood hurled all the way, a scruffy ringside worker handed a card to the card girl. She hoisted it over her head announcing "Round 9" to everyone. The card girl strutted her stuff to the four corners of the ring. The Hispanic fighter was obviously disregarding his cornerman's advice in favor of pre-round eye candy. The cornerman slapped his fighter to regain his attention, which he obediently gave. The ring card girl plastered on a fake smile as hoots and catcalls assaulted her ears. Her sleek, athletic legs almost rubbed against each other as she moved this way and that around the ring.

This woman had John Fetaccini absolutely captivated. His eyes didn't leave her for a second. Well, except for that moment when a rowdy fan bumped into him. But other than that, both eyes were on the ring card girl. She met John's gaze and winked at him so suggestively that it would have turned any teenage boy watching into a puddle of prepubescent goo.

Having made the loop, the ring card girl lowered the card and bent beneath the ring, accidentally giving a father and young son at ringside way too much of an eyeful of her chest. "Don't tell your mom about this," the older man uneasily warned his child.

John stood out of his seat and followed after this girl as she wandered into the rear of the stadium. The bell rang once more and the two fighters resumed their violent war for the clamoring fans.

In the back aisles of Klaude Stadium, the ring card girl carried non-sequential numbered cards, heading for a dressing room. She looked emotionally tapped, as if she wanted to be somewhere, anywhere, but there. Her high-heeled footfalls actually overpowered the crowd's cheering, echoing off the aisle's walls. Thus was the end of the work day for Cora Secillia, street walkin' woman.

As Cora made her way to the dressing room door, a coat-sleeved arm reached out and opened it for her. It, of course, belonged to John. Cora didn't even look up at him before halfway mumbling, "Thanks. Not interested. Not supposed to be back here. Yadda, yadda, yadda," and waving him off. She spoke in a soft, shy manner without any discernible accent.

John scoffed loud enough to make sure Cora heard it. She looked up to see who it was and her mood and facial expression immediately 180'ed. And as proof, she jumped at John in an embrace.

"Oh John, I'm so glad you're here!" she cheered.

"Hey, me too," John retorted.

Their hug stayed together a little longer than one might expect, but finally Cora pulled away, dragging her fingers across the sides of John's face.

"I gotta change," she meekly explained. "Wait for me here?" she seemed to beg.

"Everything looks great from here," John said, eying Cora's exposed cleavage. "I understand why you gotta change, but whatever..." he shrugged.

Cora groped herself. "Because I don't want to freeze these off on the walk home," she smirked. "Don't worry, John," she continued as she walked into the dressing room. "I'll put it back on later."

John almost began to follow, but the door swung shut in his face. He pulled back and with dull surprise proclaimed, "Yay."

The city sidewalk was lit up by street lights placed intermittently. Some had burned out every so often and had yet to be replaced. Fortunately, the wind-blown trash and rain had died down.

John and Cora headed for home, their hands locked together swinging as they walked. Cora was now far more sensibly clothed, garbed in a dark blue and black-striped button-up shirt and a pressed black skirt that made her radiate intelligence and loveliness. She carried a brown purse around her right shoulder that wasn't quite designer quality, but did its job nicely. The change from Ring Card Cora to Street Cora was completed with a pair of narrow, thin-rimmed glasses so she could see much better.

"You wanna go eat someplace?" John queried. Cora's stomach growled in response. "I'd call that a big yes," John said taken aback.

"Do I want to? Yes," Cora explained. "Can we afford it? No."

"Ah, that's no problem, honey," John shot back. "We'll just dine and dash. Besides—"

"I am way too tired for a dine and dash, John," Cora interrupted. "When we get home, I'll make us something."

"As you wish, baby," John said, hoping each time she'd get the reference. And she did, each time replying with an appreciative grin.

"So what'd you think?" Cora asked, assuming they were on the same wavelength.

"'Bout what?" John queried.

"The fight," the young lady explained.

"Wait, there was a fight?" John feigned ignorance.

"MMA title match," Cora rolled her eyes. "We just came from there! Thought you guys loved all that macho stuff?"

"I wasn't there for the fight," John scoffed. "I come to see you."

"So how'd I do?" Cora inquired.

"You were definitely hot, Cora," John responded, meaning every word of it. "And I definitely knew it was the ninth round."

"Mmm... I always feel like such a bimbo when I'm up there," Cora revealed. "I wish I could quit."

"So quit," John recommended.

"C'mon, John. You know we need the money," Cora defended.

"Do you really wanna do something you don't like doin' for a few extra bucks?" John asked.

"A few extra bucks?" Cora scoffed. "I got a hun'nerd extra big boys in my purse, John!"

"See? I knew we could afford dinner out," John gestured with his loose hand.

"Yeah... or we could pay the electric bill," Cora threw on the wet blanket.

"Fine. Hide behind your fancy logic," John groaned.

"Besides," Cora continued, "if I thought I could make some money singing *It's Raining Men*, you'd better break out the hip-waders, my friend."

John chuckled and the two lovebirds tightened their fingers around each other's hands.

A door with "101" emblazoned across it in copper-colored numbers swung open. Following a dull click, the darkness in the room receded in a flash. It was an apartment, though not much of one. Lamps, tables, a stuffing-exposed sofa, a tube television, and a radio could be seen in the immediate area. Despite the serious low-rent atmosphere, it had a very homey vibe to it.

John made a beeline for the kitchen as Cora followed, locking the door behind her. She set her purse down on the dining table before disdainfully kicking her shoes away. As her feet were released from their daily bondage, she let out a content sigh.

John appeared, brandishing a bottle of orange juice. "Want somethin' ta drink?" he offered.

"Not yet," Cora replied as she leaned against the table. "Thanks, though."

John took a swig from the bottle.

"Don't drink from the bottle, John," Cora chided. John wiped his mouth then gave an apologetic shrug before putting it back into the fridge. Cora walked away and plopped down on the couch, wiped out from the day's work. Before long, though, she reached out and grabbed something to read off her lamp stand where a pile of books and magazines had been stacked like a doctor's waiting room. John, meanwhile, headed down a short hall into the back.

The bedroom was as spartan as the living room. There were chairs, a table and vanity, a dresser with clock radio, and bed, all of which looked old and worn. On the wall was a framed photo of John and Cora, strategically hung to cover up what appeared to be a hole in the wall. A curtain blotted out the room's only window to the outside.

As John entered, he switched on the lights and threw his coat over a chair before he sat down at the vanity. He stared into the mirror as if he expected someone else to be there. After a few moments of watching, John began to fidget with his face, pushing it this way and that as if to change it like silly putty. Giving up on that fool's errand, he brushed matted black hair out of his face with his fingers.

"How did it all come to this?" John thought to himself. *"Every decision I ever made was the wrong one. How am I ever gonna make something of myself with that wrap sheet?"* After a

moment, John craned his neck around. "*Well, that's not true. I did do one thing right.*"

John then got up and headed for his draped coat, riffling through its pockets.

Cora was still in the living room reading some Anne Rice. She fidgeted slightly before adjusting her position. "*Ow,*" she thought before muttering aloud, "Damned springs."

John came up behind Cora and began to massage her shoulders as she read. Cora responded with an appreciative groan.

"Ohhh, that feels sooooooo good," Cora encouraged. "I gotta work at the Lodge tomorrow. I don't want to. Don't make me go to work, John," she begged like a kid wanting to stay home from school.

"Okay, don't," John told her, unsure of her intentions. "Stay here. We'll have a snow day. We can make a couch fort..."

Cora grinned at the idea. "That actually sounds like a lot of fun," she admitted.

John bent down, resting his chin on the back of Cora's couch. "Lookie what I got for ya," he teased.

"If this is another Ginsu knife that cuts through lead pipes and tomatoes, you can forget it," Cora dismissively said. "Those things won't cut hot butter."

John produced the cash he scammed on the street and handed it over to Cora. She set her book down and took note. "Where'd you get this?" she wondered aloud.

"Just workin' a little overtime, baby," John half-truthed. "Thought you could use it."

Cora angled up to give a grateful cheek kiss. "It's cold. I want a Snuggie," she randomly spoke up.

"Well, you can get one now, can'tcha?" John stated more than asked.

"Touché," Cora smirked.

"How about a snuggle instead?" John offered.

Cora lit up as John moved around to her side of the couch and sat down facing her. Cora clamped her arms around John like a worried baby.

"I don't care how comfy they're supposed to be; Snuggies will never take the place of a good snuggle," Cora declared.

"I dunno," John replied. "Isn't it like a big blanket that's like 'Uh-uh. I'mma keep you warm'?"

"Isn't that what you're doing right now?" Cora inquired.

"Man, you are on fire tonight, Cora," John admitted. Cora smiled as she buried her head in John's chest. She could hear the beating of his tell-tale heart through his clothes. Slowly, John leaned over backwards into a reclined position where Cora was lying on top of him.

"Why are we moving this way?" Cora asked unsure about the slow, yet sudden movement.

"If we go the other way, I'll squash you," John explained.

"Mmm. Let's do this for half an hour or so and then I'll call us in a pizza with this new money," Cora said as if she was falling asleep. "How's that sound, honey?"

"A half an hour?" John mock whined. "But I'm hungry now!"

Suddenly it hit the dirty side of Cora's mind. "I'll put on tonight's outfit for you, John," Cora cooed in her best seductive voice.

"What do I get for two hours of this?" John bargained.

"Fuck that!" Cora exclaimed. "In two hours, I'll have starved to death." The two laughed.

"A half hour it is," John relented, kissing the top of Cora's head.

CHAPTER TWO - A Hard Night's Journey Into Day

Grimy water trickled into a gross, brown puddle on a cement floor. This basement or whatever it was stretched like a bricky sewer down corridors and pathways under the city. The distant sound of sobs and raucous laughter grew louder and louder with each turn of the bricked corners. Vehicles were easily heard driving overhead.

In the very back reaches of this area, a gang of toughs drank liquor while loudly carrying on amongst each other. They were dressed to the nines in thuggish tastelessness. Bling. Vests with no shirts underneath. Sagging pants. The works.

In the middle of this congregation of delinquency, was Cora, tied to an old, wooden chair, sobbing pathetically. Her arms were tightly pulled and bound behind her back with a thick, splintery-looking rope. Her delicate face was smudged with bruises. Tears had smeared her eyeliner like liquid thrown onto a painting. Her hair was disheveled and her clothes ripped into disarray in an obvious effort to get a better look at her generous goods.

"Please," Cora meekly cooed. "Let me go. I promise I won't tell anyone. Not even John."

The gang's reaction was only that of laughter. Some of them even mocked her pleas. One tough, dressed in a loose, orange hoodie and blue baggy parachute pants with an obnoxious blonde-dyed Mohawk swigged down a mouthful of booze before turning to their quarry.

"We're not too worried about that," the mohawk explained. "See, we made sure that guy John didn't get any ideas and interrupt our little session here. So, he's, uh... what, met with an accident?"

More laughter broke out from these hooligans. Cora would be angry at them if her heart wasn't too busy cracking in half. "Oh, John," she whimpered as she clinched her eyes and more tears streamed down her aching face.

"Okay, okay," said another punk, this one wearing a pair of sunglasses and dressed in nothing but suspenders holding up a pair of baggy pants that still managed to sag far too low. "Let's get this show on the road!" he commanded as he threw his beer can clattering to the floor.

The others shouted forth a roar of approval and as if en masse, they turned their menacing attention to Cora. Looking up from the depths of despair, Cora noticed them closing in on her, gulping her fear down and biting her lip. She writhed about ineffectually in the chair but it was no use. Her eyes widened as she saw them start to disrobe or otherwise expose themselves. The gang's shadow completely eclipsed over the helpless Cora as they...

Cora jolted straight up from her bed, wide awake out of a dead sleep. She sucked down air like she'd been held underwater for five minutes, her eyes almost bulging out of their sockets as sweat glittered across her forehead and shoulders. Her light blue strapped nightgown was wet and disheveled. Looking around the room in panic, she realized she was back in her bedroom. Immediately, she spied the empty pizza box on the nearby table but right next to her was John, obliviously asleep. Asleep and safe.

"John?" Cora quietly broke the sound of a train passing in the far distance. But there was no response to be had. Not even the classic snoring.

"John?" she queried again. Still nothing.

Cora slowly laid back down amid the rumpled covers. She then clutched onto John's back like a frightened child, burying her head into his night shirt.

"Please don't leave me, John," she whispered.

The sun gleamed as it rose across the cityscape of Klaude, turning the run-down buildings a faux shade of gold. Other than its glorious morning color, the city didn't look as if it was nearly as ready to wake up as the sun was.

In John and Cora's bedroom, John was still asleep, dressed in his unkempt bedclothes. Slight humming permeated across the apartment. It eventually grabbed John's attention, pulling him back to the waking world. His head slowly turned to look around. In his blurred line of sight, he saw Cora moving to and fro exiting and re-entering the bedroom as she prepared for work. She was clad only in an undone, white dress shirt that hung down to her thighs. She swigged from a glass of orange juice as she moved about.

"Hey, Cora..." John yawned. He obviously wasn't used to being up so early. Cora stopped, taking note of the event, before sitting down to look over a pair of neatly-pressed black dress slacks.

"So finally decide to wake up, Nightingale?" she kidded.

"What's the difference between a jeweler and a jailor?" John inquired.

Cora thought it over a second before giving up with a shrug and another drink of juice. "I don't know. What?"

"One sells watches," John explained. "The other watches cells." The poor joke amused John. And Cora too apparently as she chuckled, though she was ashamed that it did.

"Oh, get away from me," she chided, smiling despite herself.

John lay down and went back to sleep as Cora went back about getting ready for the day.

About three hours later, John came around the corner into the kitchen, dressed up in duplicates of his same street finery from the night before. The low sound of vehicles passing by and dogs barking invaded the apartment in a muffled form from outside. John headed over to the fridge and took a swig of milk from the jug. He wiped the bottle mouth clean before placing it back and shutting the door. He then turned to the nearby kitchen counter, finding a note written in hurried cursive.

"Sweetheart, Breakfast is in the microwave. Warm it up before you go out. Try to mop the kitchen if you get a chance. Something's sticky. Ick."

The note was signed with a kiss in lipstick. John made his way over to the microwave. It looked as if it were passed its prime 20 years ago. How it was still working today was anyone's guess. A bottle of syrup sat on the top, along with a clutter of change. Mostly pennies. John opened the microwave to reveal a plate of bacon and Belgian waffles inside. He activated the microwave and it loudly roared to life as its inner light blazed on.

CHAPTER THREE - Work Day

The early sun still gave everything a luminous golden look. John Fetaccini headed with purpose for parts unknown, each footfall of his scuffed military boots slightly audible. A handful of people would pass by going the other way, but none of them paid him much notice. One man, a miscreant by the name of Hornsby dressed in a coat with a fur collar, was coming John's way and he took notice.

"Hey, Hornsby..." John began. "You behavin' yourself?" he punctuated by pointing his hand into the shape of a gun.

"Sure, John," Hornsby nervously answered. "You know I am."

"Alright," John responded. Both men continued on their merry ways.

Along a sidewalk nearby, a trio of high school-aged ruffians by the names of Harry, Jerry, and Tom headed ostensibly to school, but in reality, who knows where their trip to a waste of an education would take them. They catcalled at women of various ages as they passed by. Some were half-assed attempts at being cute and others were downright obscene.

A lone water bottle sitting next to a telephone pole with a couple of yellow roses inside came to the unfortunate attention of Harry.

"Look at this stupid bottle," Harry pointed out.

"Yeah, they couldn't even afford a vase!" Tom chided, oddly pronouncing the word with an "ah" sound. "What a loser!"

As they walked by, Jerry meanspirtedly kicked over the bottle, sending the water inside and the roses spilling out across the concrete sidewalk. For reasons known only to themselves, this elicited mischievous laughter from the three.

John suddenly rounded a corner from a nearby alley and immediately spied the destroyed monument.

"'Ey!" he shouted. "You kids do this?" he pointed at the downed bottle.

Harry, Jerry, and Tom stopped in their tracks. They turned and gave their best hard looks, picking a poor time to cement their status as idiot kids.

"So what if we did?" Harry barked.

"What's it to ya?" Jerry snipped.

"You know why these flowers are there?" John asked.

"Some idiot's trying to plant shit in the concrete," Jerry sneered.

With a burst of subdued anger, John closed the gap between himself and the kids. They were too stupid to get away from there.

"That what they teachin' you in school?" John began. "No, a rose is here 'cuz somebody got mugged or knifed or shot here."

"So?" Harry shrugged.

"So, put a sock in it, lard-ass!" Tom spoke up, irritably.

John reached out and grabbed a hold of Tom by the collar and dragged him over to the downed bottle, pushing the boy's head down near it like a bad puppy.

"Ain't yer mother taught you any respect?" John lectured. "This person died and somebody loves 'em enough ta leave flowers for 'em and you just come and knock 'em over... what the hell's wrong with yous?!"

"It wasn't me!" Tom strained. "It-It was Jerry!"

"You little punk!" Jerry furiously growled.

"I don't care who it was!" John yelled. "Fix it!"

Tom dutifully began to scoop up the roses and righted the bottle once more. John's clamped fist let go of Tom's collar and the boy fled the scene, closely followed by Harry and Jerry.

"Watch your ass," John waved cheerfully. He then made the sign of the cross over the bottle of roses before moving on his way.

The so-called Puptown Gentlemen's Club looked like anything but. It was a seedy little building tucked just off the street down a wide alley between and behind two other street-side buildings that one wouldn't even look at twice. Truth be told, any gentleman worth his salt wouldn't be caught dead here.

John came around the corner from the nearby street. A gang of toughs congregated outside greeted John cheerfully as he closed in on them. John returned their greetings before passing through and entering the building.

If the outside of the Puptown Gentlemen's Club was nothing to write home about, the inside was even less worth mentioning. It was populated with several tough-looking people inside. There were sparsely decorated card tables and folding chairs that seemed to be the extent of the furniture. The biggest expense was spared on whatever Wal-Mart run that got them all this. A pool game in a smoky corner caused the noise of slamming pool balls to echo across the room. The craggy walls didn't have much of note other than some newspaper clippings tacked to the wall and—oddly enough—a framed autographed picture of Stephen Colbert, raising his eyebrow and giving a thumbs-up.

Sarrageno Incognito and Dan Clemens sat at a table next to the door. "Geno" was the taller of the two with a short, but full head of hair and beady eyes. Clemens was shorter and fatter, almost a meaner-looking Danny DeVito. He fidgeted with his cell phone. They both gave the idea of low-rent *Sopranos* rejects. The door swung open and John entered.

"Hey John!" Sarrageno shot off.

"How's tricks?" Clemens kidded, not even looking up.

"'Ey guys," John replied automatically. "Cicci in?"

"Yeah," Clemens hitched a thumb back, still working with his cell in the other hand. "He's in back somewheres."

"Thanks," John answered.

John left the two and passed through the mostly concrete room. Several other people sat at tables, talking things over but what they were saying could only be heard by them. Some of them took notice of John and greeted him as walked by.

Eventually, John made his way to the back of the room where several people sat around one table. It was just a little nicer than the other tables in the joint. The most important man in this group went by the name of Cicci Colone. He was in his early forties with slicked-back brown hair, and dressed in a nice, but casual brown suit with matching vest and overcoat. Beside him sat his driver, Dimi, a squat little rat of a man, wearing a grey trilby and dark sunglasses even though he was inside. The two appeared to be discussing something important.

John slid into an empty chair near Cicci. "Hey Cicci," he began.

Cicci turned to acknowledge the sound.

"Yo, John!" Cicci replied, genuinely happy to see him. "How ya doin' this fine autumn day?"

"Can't complain; every day above ground is a good day," John said in a merry manner. "Got anything for me today?"

"Dimi was just tellin' me there's some jag-off that ain't paid up on a loan for six weeks now," Cicci said, hitching his thumb towards his driver.

"Way ahead a' you," John said. He pulled out a notepad and pen from the inner pockets of his overcoat. "Who am I lookin' for?"

"Seth Bindle," Cicci began. "Young kid. Works stocking shelves over at Harold's. Got blonde hair, about

6'2. Needed money for an engagement ring... or somethin'."

John wrote the details in his pad. "Seth Bindle... blonde hair... ring," John muttered to himself. "Oh, I remember him. He was the one with the moles on his face, right?"

"Nah, you're thinking of Sammerson on the west side," Cicci corrected. "This kid came in with a ball cap and 500-dollar sneakers." Nearby, Dimi's expression seemed to want John gone as soon as possible.

"500-dollar sneakers?!" John asked incredulously. "If I paid 500 dollars for something, I'd have to live in it! Alright, I'm taking Geno and Clemens and..." John looked around the room. "Where's Vinelli?"

"Vinelli's sick," Cicci explained. "He's got some baaaaad shit. Swine flu or somethin'. He's gonna be out for a few days."

John exhaled in exasperation. "Okay, Geno and Clemens'll have ta do," he said in resignation. "How much he owe you?"

"325 bucks, I think," Cicci scratched his head. "Hell, I can't remember," he shrugged. "Dimi, do you know?"

"It's $350, Boss," the driver responded.

"350," John repeated. "Got it. Back later."

Almost as fast as he appeared, John set off towards the entrance again. Eventually, he made his way back to the table Sarrageno and Clemens were sitting at.

"Come on, guys," John said, patting one of Geno's shoulders. "Time to go to work!" John then opened and held the door for them as Geno and Clemens stood up and exited. Clemens was still fidgeting with his phone.

Harold's Groceries was just an average, everyday grocery store in the middle of the city. The pavement in the parking lot was cracked and in bad need of repair. An overturned shopping cart lie between the parking lot and the nearby street. Another cart rolled inconspicuously into traffic. Early morning shoppers exited with their bags of groceries.

The stock room in the back of the store was even less appealing than the outside. It was dark and dingy and generally unpleasant to look at. Spilt liquids of indeterminate origin caked the floor. It was a wonder the place was even still in operation.

Seth Bindle, the young man Cicci was after, loaded crate after crate of eggs onto a roller. If we didn't know better, one might think it was Easter. Seth loaded up the last crate of the bunch with a groan. Turning back, he found John with Geno and Clemens in tow, standing nearby as if they'd just ninja-ed into the store.

Seth didn't know exactly who John was, but he knew he was trouble. His eyes widened just before he ran off in the opposite direction. John immediately gave chase after him down the dank hallway.

After what was only a surprisingly short amount of time, John caught up to Seth and threw him against the wooden wall, causing it to rattle loudly behind them.

"Lemme go!" Seth protested.

"Shut it!" John barked. He shook the young man by his collar. "You might *think* you know who I am, but I *know* who you are," John explained. "Cicci wants the money you owe him... NOW."

"Cicci?" Seth asked, unconvincingly. "Who's Cicci?" Sarrageno and Clemens responded with a roll of their eyes. John, however, was less ambivalent, and smacked Seth in the forehead.

"Don't play games with me. No time for it, baby," John angrily declared. "Cicci says you pay me $350 or I make you bleed. Your call."

Seth breathed sharply. His eyes darted across the room. He suddenly pointed. "Look! A distraction!" he called out, completely deadpan.

John whirled around to look, giving Seth just enough time to break free and make a run for it. John immediately realized his folly and threw his arms into the air in frustration.

"John, you gotta stop fallin' for that," Clemens reprimanded. The three collectors took pursuit as fast as their questionable bodies could move them.

The back door to the rear lot swung open and Seth emerged from the darkness within. He tried to put as much distance between him and the store as he could, but John and the other two eventually pushed their way out the door as well. John stepped forward and then whipped out his pistol, firing off a couple of shots. They hit the pavement, causing sparks to fly out of the ground just shy of Seth's running feet. Seth slowed down and eventually came to an exhausted halt.

"Get the fuck over here!" John yelled, gesturing for the kid to get his ass back over to them. Seth slowly began the trek back to the collectors.

"The fuck are you doin', John?!" Sarrageno demanded to know. "You wanna get us pinched?!"

"Did you wanna go after 'im?" John retorted, gesturing to the approaching young man.

"Well... no, not really," Geno stammered.

"Then shut the fuck up," John hissed in his gravelly voice.

Seth had finally made his way back to the three men. He breathed heavily and his face had turned a flush red.

"Where's the fire, yo?" Seth nonchalantly asked.

"First off," John began, "'Yo' is slang for 'Hello' or 'Hey' or 'Hi'. You don't put 'yo' at the end of a sentence. It'd be like sayin' 'How's it goin', hi'?"

"We ain't in no English class here," Seth observed.

"Anything worth doin's worth doin' right," John shot back. "Three-hun'nerd an' fifty cherry trees... NOW," he demanded, his demeanor suddenly harder than seconds before.

With a huff, Seth fished money out of his pockets. But as soon as the boy pulled it out, John yanked the bills away and began to count it. He followed that by holding out the cash at Seth and slapping him in the head.

"This isn't enough," John mumbled, looking over the money. He then noticed something off about the bills... "Is this Monopoly money?!" Sure enough, mixed in with the real bills were some colorful Monopoly dollar bills. "Are you lookin' to get pistol-whipped, kid?"

Seth fished out more money and handed it over. John took it and counted it off. He seemed mollified.

"Yeah, I thought so," the collector snarled. "Next time pay on time... ya folla?"

John backed away a few steps, putting his pistol back beneath his overcoat.

"Yeah," Seth said between breaths, legitimately scared. "Yeah, I follow."

"Good doin' business with ya," John said, punctuating it with a click of his tongue and a finger gun. He turned to walk away, motioning for Sarrageno and Clemens to follow suit. The two hooligans gave Seth the evil eye before following John around the corner of the store.

Back at the Gentlemen's Club, Cicci sat at a table going over some monetary figures with a pencil and pad. Suddenly, the $350 he requested was placed directly in front of him. Cicci slowly looked up the arm holding it, finding that it belonged to John. A warm smile crept across Cicci's face.

"John!" the boss cheered. "Good job, my man!" He took the wad of cash from his underling.

"I wouldn't trust that guy with any other loans, Cicci," John reported. "He was a runner. But I foreclosed on him if ya know what I mean... and I think you do."

"Ah, don't worry about it, Johnny." Cicci said, admiring the roll of money. "We got the money back. That's the main thing."

Cicci counted off 35 dollars and gave it to John before rolling up the remaining money and sticking it in a back pocket. John similarly pocketed his percentage of the take.

"Siddown, John," Cicci said. John slid into a nearby empty chair.

"What's yer schedule this week?" Cicci queried, pronouncing "schedule" in the Queen's English.

"Not a helluva lot," John said. "Why?"

"Well, there are some people I know that need your help," Cicci explained.

"What's the pay?" John inquired.

"A grand," Cicci replied.

"A thousand dollars?" John clarified.

"Don't repeat everything I say," Cicci ordered, pointing at John. "Look, it's a simple job. Guy needs some help and thinks you're the guy that can give it to him."

"That doesn't sound remotely gay," John teased. "You didn't find this guy on Craigslist didja?" Cicci's only response was an annoyed, implied facepalm. "I'll think about it," John quickly followed.

"Don't think, do," Cicci said. "John, we can't let ya go soft on us. What do you want to be remembered around here as?"

"John Fetaccini, the world's greatest sex machine," he explained. "With a coffee mug to prove it." Cicci actually laughed in response, shaking his head in spite of himself.

"Look, if you wanna be my successor, you're gonna have to tighten up," Cicci informed. "The guy frequents the bar out west a' town. Give me a call cause they're waitin'."

"Hey, you know I ain't got no phone, Cicci," John humbly replied.

"Just tell me, John, okay?" Cicci replied, losing patience.

"Okay, I'll go see 'em," John relented. "You know this gun's for hire... even if we are just dancin' in the dark."

"Good," Cicci chuckled. "And knock that shit off. It's not funny."

"You're laughin'," John pointed out.

"Okay, maybe it's a little funny," Cicci admitted.

John looked around the room. "Where's Dimi, Cicci?" he wondered.

"Out fuckin' Cora," the driver's voice said out of nowhere.

John shot to his feet in an instantaneous furious rage when Cicci raised his hands in intervention.

"Hey Dimi, knock that shit off right now," the boss chided. "Now, that *ain't* funny."

Dimi chuckled to himself in a misguided rebellion before he sat down beside Cicci. "Was to me," he whispered.

John noticed the pencil-to-pad figuring Cicci was engaged in. "What are you so busy with over there?" he asked.

"Ah, doin' my damned taxes," Cicci replied. "It's the devil's own work."

"You do your own taxes?" John asked. "Isn't that dangerous?"

"You want to know what's dangerous?" Cicci pointed out. "A government stiff askin' me where I got a sudden 30,000 dollar spike."

"Can't say I disagree with that," John replied.

"Damned skippy," Cicci said. "Alright, get the hell outta here, John. You're screwin' up my figurin'. We'll come getcha if we need ya any more today."

John stood up, but bent over toward the notepad. "That should be an eight," John pointed out. Cicci reacted with an irritated groan as John moved off across the room.

The Fountainstone Lodge was a massive-looking place. A monster amongst buildings in town and very ritzy to boot. The outdoor colors were shades of red and white, but done in a way that wasn't aggressive on the eyes to look at. It had the vague architecture of a southern Big House. John walked along a nearby sidewalk heading straight for the swanky lodge. A pair of sliding automatic glass doors parted for him as he entered.

In the kitchen, waiters and waitresses bused food to and from as chefs in the back cooked it up as fast and good as they could. The waiters were all dressed alike in some combination of white dress shirt with tie and black slacks to try to add a classy ambience to the place. The ensembles varied in exactness from person to person, though.

In a nook across the busy cookery were Cora and another, homelier waitress talking amongst each other. The waitress smoked a cigarette as she stood directly beneath a sign reading "*No Smoking.*" Cora had on a short, black tie ending in two blades underneath her flat collar. Her compatriot did not.

"...And then I woke up," Cora explained. "It was the scariest dream I've ever had in my life. Ever."

"Sounds pretty fuckin' wild," the waitress grinned, apparently focusing on the wrong idea. "Wouldn't mind being on the other end of that."

"Wait, what?" Cora asked, not sure she heard that.

"What?" the waitress shot back. "Did you tell John about it?"

"No, it's just a stupid dream," Cora groaned. "I didn't want to bother him with it."

"Well it's not stupid if it bothered you this much," the waitress retorted.

"Well..." Cora thought aloud, "I don't know. I might bring it up later."

"Listen," the waitress said, smoke flowing from her mouth. "Next time this happens, just lie back and think of England."

"'Next time'?" Cora asked. "What?"

"What?" the waitress shot back again. A bell suddenly began to ring repeatedly. Cora whirled around towards its direction. Standing across from them was an angry burly chef, bent over the small bell.

"Cora!" the chef growled. "Meal goin' out, come ahhhhhhhhn!"

Cora and the waitress gave each other "back to the grind" looks before the prettier of the two headed over to pick up a massive tray of food.

"Don't dream anything I wouldn't dream," the waitress offered.

Cora hoisted the tray off the counter like a pro.

"I'll try not," Cora answered.

The dining room was filled with smallish round tables, peppered with diners. Most of them were older people. Some couples; no young people. John entered in the very back and clocked the room. After a second or two, he snaked his way through and exited out a door which led to the kitchen with none of the diners the wiser.

Cora carried the tray of food on one hand as she hauled a fold-out table under her arm. She glided most carefully over to a table where an elderly couple by the name of Smitts sat. The husband looked like he'd just came back from a round of golf while the wife appeared as if she'd gone out for drinks.

"Here you are, Mr. and Mrs. Smitts," Cora said as she set up the diners' meal before them. "Just smell that corn." The couple looked suitably appeased with the foodstuffs as Cora spread it out before them.

"Is there anything else I can get you?" Cora asked.

"Iiiiii think we're good here," Mr. Smitts replied.

"Great. Just yell for me if you need anything more," Cora informed.

"Oh, he will," Mrs. Smitts spoke up.

"Well... don't yell," Cora clarified, "but... you know what I mean," she smiled. "Enjoy your meal."

The Smitts sat about eating their dinner as Cora turned and headed back to the kitchen doors. Her fake servers' smile immediately dropped from her face.

Cora entered the kitchen, dusting food residue off her servers' vest. She then headed for the next meal to be carried out. As she turned a corner, she found John hidden there.

"Hey, sweetie," John announced himself.

"Oh hi, John," Cora said, looking up. "What're you doing here?"

"Eh, it's boring at home," he answered with a shrug.

"That's not the only place," Cora said with a huff. "Did you mop the kitchen floor?"

"It's dryin' as we speak," John lied through his teeth. "What time you comin' home tonight?" he asked, quickly changing the subject.

Cora thought for a minute as servers milled about behind her.

"Uh, I was thinkin' of workin' for about another hour," she calculated. "Then I'll clock out an' come home."

"Can I walk you home?" the collector queried.

"Yeah, sure," Cora said, not really paying attention to what she was saying.

"I'll just hang around here till then, if ya don't mind," John justified. "Keep all the riffraff from botherin' ya."

Cora gave a coy smile to John that seemed to convey the thought *"like you?"* She then headed for the next tray of food to be hauled out. John followed her through the kitchen, looking at the various meals set up for consumption.

"Light day today," John spoke up.

"What happened?" Cora questioned.

"Some punk was tryin' ta cheat us outta some cash an' made a run for it," John explained. "So we had to do some convincin' to get 'im back in line. You know, nothin' new."

"I can imagine how you did that," Cora replied, looking over a tray.

"Fries are up!" the chef yelled from behind the counter. Cora headed over toward the voice like Pavlov's dog.

"Oh, John!" Cora exclaimed. "I want to go see a movie this weekend... *The U.P.S. vs. the Federal Express*. It looks so funny."

"I haven't heard of that," John retorted. "I don't trust that title either. Will Ferrell's not in it, is he? Cause God help you if he is."

"Yeah, yeah, I remember the *Anchorman 2* fiasco," Cora waved him off. "No, it's got Stallone and Schwarzenegger. Bruce Willis might be in it too."

"I... am cautiously curious," John owned up to it. He then suddenly began to speak in Ah-nold's voice... or at least as well as someone with his raspy voice could. "Ah'll be bahk... I have a few more packages for you in de trahk," John spoke in the Terminator's cadence.

Cora giggled in response. She then began to mutter as Rocky Balboa. "'Ey yo!" Cora cheerily said before muttering something incoherently and wrapping it up with "sign here."

John and Cora laughed amongst each other at their little impromptu skit.

On a basketball court in the Proton part of town, a group of young athletically-fit men played a game of hoops while hip-hop bumped from a stereo nearby. The men half-shouted raucously to one another as they shot for the basket or hurled the ball from one side of the court to the other. Despite the loudness of the communication, it was nothing more than a friendly game to pass the time, not some contest of dominance over one another.

Off sides, a trio of black men sat around each other on the benches. On one side was Jerome Marks, the youngest of the three. He was spindly and twitchy with an air of something-to-prove about him. On the other side was Ty Briggs, an older-looking kid with dreads and a mouth full of golden choppers. He looked like a bodyguard of sorts, but more easy-going in demeanor.

The oldest of the three—28 to be exact—was dressed in a due rag and a baggy tank top. He was smart, cautious, and a bona fide B.M.F known as Crimilicious, the Prince of Proton. His right eyebrow had a shave mark through it and a fade shaved into his hair on both sides of his face.

"Man, when he gonna get here?" Jerome complained. "He's ten minutes late!"

"Patience, Jerome," Ty warned with an outstretched hand. "He'll show... if he knows what's good for 'im."

"Ty's right, dawg," Crimilicious interjected. "Not everybody has 'eir watch set da same. Don't be shady."

A younger white man by the name of Roy dressed in jorts and a ball cap appeared nearby. He walked with trepidation, carrying a nondescript, brown paper bag in his hand. Crimilicious looked up and took note of his arrival.

"Roy, my man!" Crimilicious spoke up. "I knew you'd be here."

"Sorry 'bout that," Roy replied, rubbing the back of his neck. "I was a little nervous."

"Ain't no need for anyone workin' for Crimilicious to be nervous," the boss man explained. "You get our stuff?"

"Right here," Roy said as he handed the bag over. "My sister threatened to call the police but a couple of pimp slaps put that bitch in her place, ya knawwhutI'msayin'?

"I heeeeard dat," Jerome agreed.

Crimilicious opened and looked inside the paper bag. He then turned and handed it over to Ty. Roy looked on, fidgeting nervously.

"What you think?" Crimilicious asked Ty for thoughts.

Ty opened the bag and inspected its contents, moving his head around to see what was inside.

"A good 30, 40K, easy bro," Ty concluded.

"I-I did good?" Roy queried.

"You did alright, lil man," Crimilicious nodded.

The larger boss man stood up and gave Roy a man hug, a token of appreciation, but pulled away before Roy could return it. Crimilicious pulled out a rolled-up sock-sized wad of cash and counted out an appropriate amount before handing it over to Roy. The younger man sighed to himself in relief.

"Let's roll, ya'll," Crimilicious announced, causing Jerome and Ty to spring to their feet. "I'll see ya, Roy."

Their "stuff" in tow, Jerome and Ty turned to head off. Crimilicious suddenly stopped short in his tracks.

"Yo, Roy!" he bellowed out.

Roy halted with a frightened grimace. He slowly turned back around.

"Don't be no jerk-ass..." Crimilicious spoke to Roy, not facing him. "Take ya sista out somewhere nice, dig?"

"Oh," Roy replied. "Yes, of course! Later, Crim!"

"Lata, blood," the boss man answered before continuing on his way once more. His boys followed suit, headed back for the neighborhood streets and apparently uninterested in the results of the basketball game behind them.

CHAPTER FOUR - Bad Blood and Something Sticky

Cicci's four-door, mid-70's Ford drifted across a rickety backstreet of Puptown. The thing was dingy and dirty and looked rundown, likely from overuse. Dents were poked all over the thing and it was obvious somebody had even keyed the thing.

Dimi drove while Cicci sat shotgun, writing notes on a piece of paper.

"We got a few more errands an' that'll be it for today," Cicci instructed.

"You got it, Boss," Dimi replied.

"Hey, did we collect from McElroy?" Cicci queried.

"I dunno," Dimi said with a shrug.

"I think we did," Cicci thought aloud. "Eh, I'll look into it later. Hey! Swing over to Fryers' place. We'll pick up John after he's done collectin'."

"Ya know, I don't know why you keep that street kid aroun'," Dimi grumbled. "He's a wild card."

"A wild card is exactly the ace in the hole you need to stay on top of things," Cicci explained. "Besides, he's loyal as hell and tougher than twisted cougar shit. You have somebody like that with you and a lot of roadblocks go away. I wouldn't wanna be workin' *against* him, I'll tell ya that!"

Dimi scoffed dismissively.

"What was that?" Cicci raised an eyebrow.

"Sorry," Dimi coughed. "Some phlegm."

The Fryers' place looked like a prime example of a crack house if there ever was one—a degenerate's degenerate home. The thing was falling apart. Planks of wood had fallen to the wayside. The whole roof needed re-shingling, as evidenced by the many shingles lying on the ground. The grass was grown up, but oddly enough, not everywhere, just in spots like the yard had been invaded by monster crab grass.

The inside was less to speak of. Sunlight from outside shone in and there were some spots where it looked as though one could toss a cat through the wall.

John Fetaccini was arguably having a worse time than this house was. He wove out of the way of a light stand being swung at his face. The aggressor was one Randall Fryers. He was a thin, frail-looking, wiry bastard that seemed to have just shot up some crystal meth. This guy didn't just break bad... he tossed it in pieces over the side of the Sears Tower.

"Randall, this isn't necessary!" John pleaded.

There was another swing of the light stand, but John was minutes out of its way.

"Just pay Cicci what you owe him," John reasoned, "and you can go back to..." He looked around the place, noting the junk pile with four sort-of walls around it. He wondered if the house had always been like this or if they had done some of this as a result of the ensuing fight. "...managing the city landfill?" John continued.

Fryers shouted incomprehensibly as he drew the light stand back over his head. "It's my fuckin' money! I'll spend it how I want!" Fryers tried to bring the light stand down on John, but caught it on the overwall of an entranceway, breaking the thing in half. Fryers stared at the broken plastic in his hands as John put up his hands in frustration.

Without warning, Fryers gave a rebel yell and charged ahead, throwing a furious assault of right and left punches, but the druggy was no match for John's readiness. He handily weaved out of the way of each. When an opening presented itself, John replied with right and left hooks to the body, then coupled that with a blow to the chin that sent Fryers sprawling to the floor into a heap of clutter. John walked over to where Fryers was lying, barely conscious and placed his old military boot onto his chest.

"You caught a bad case a' slow, Fryers," John explained. "Now tell me where you got Cicci's money hid before I stuff you in a barrel a' whoop-ass and drop you in the lake!"

With a sputter, Fryers weakly pointed to a dresser against a far wall. Some of the drawers were in disarray with clothes hanging out of them. "Top drawer," Fryers coughed.

John made his way over to the dresser and opened the top drawer. There was a stash of, presumably, drug money. John grabbed it and counted off however much he was owed—which wasn't really that much of the wad. The collector put the rest back before stashing his haul into a coat pocket.

"Now see how much easier that was?" John said as he turned back to Fryers. "Get it together, Randall.

Doped up and stupid is no way to go through life. Next time pay on time... ya folla?"

John then exited the room as fast as he could, his footfalls reverberating on the wooden floor. Fryers meanwhile had passed out and probably never even heard John's words of street wisdom.

Outside, the sound of barking dogs assaulted the peace of the neighborhood. John walked around the side of the house, heading for the street. He made his way to a rusty metal fence that surrounded the house and opened the gate that lead to the street ahead before turning to walk down the nearby sidewalk and away from this nightmare that was the Fryers' house.

A half-minute later, Cicci's car pulled up beside him and came to a slow stop. The window rolled down and Cicci stuck his head out.

"Hey, John!" Cicci happily greeted.

"Cicci, what're ya doin' here?" John inquired. "Checkin' up on me, eh?"

"Ehhh, we were out and about and thought we'd give you a lift," Cicci replied. "Come on. Hop in."

John walked over to the old Ford's rear door and entered into the back seat. Before John fully pulled the door shut, the car jerked ahead back on its course.

"So how'd we do?" Cicci wondered.

"Yeah, he had it," John answered. He then dug into his coat and forked over the money he scored to Cicci. Cicci set about counting the wad, which looked nowhere near worth the beating Fryers took to get it.

"Any trouble?" Cicci asked as he counted.

"Ah, hell-no-easy," John quickly said, completely playing it off.

Cicci held up a fistful of bills that John snatched and stuffed back into his coat.

"Dimi, swing over to John's place an' we'll drop 'im off," Cicci ordered. "Then we'll head back to my house so I can pick up some pills."

"Got anything else for me?" John questioned.

"Nah, 'at's it for today," Cicci answered. "Come back in tomorrow and we'll see." Recalling earlier, Cicci then bent around and faced John in the back. "Hey John, did we collect from McElroy?"

"Yeah, last week," John responded. "Had it ready with interest an' everything." John rubbed his knuckles as if they hurt. "I wish everybody paid like McElroy..."

Cicci tapped Dimi's shoulder and leaned in toward his ear. "See, Dimi?" he said, "That's why I need John around. He stays on top of this shit."

John reacted with confusion before cutting a glare at his boss' driver.

Cicci's car noisily made its way outside John's apartment complex. The back door opened up and John stepped out. Cicci rolled down the window and leaned out. "Hey, John..." he began.

"Yeah, Cicci?" John turned back to his boss.

"Remember, that Harris guy's gonna be waitin' on you in the bar tomorrow," Cicci reminded.

"Yeah, I remember," the collector said as if a teenager had just been told to do their chores.

"I heard you're goin' on a date with Cora this weekend," the boss continued.

"Yeah, we're goin' to see a movie, then question marks," John explained as he leaned onto the side of Cicci's hood like it was a park bench. "Why you so interested in our date, Big Man?"

"How much does she charge an hour?" Dimi grumbled under his breath. Cicci tapped him on the shoulder and John definitely heard it from outside. He bent into the window in front of Cicci.

"What's your damage, Dimi?" John demanded to know.

"You're my 'damage', creep," Dimi shot back.

"Well, why don't you do somethin' about it instead a' actin' like a passive-aggressive lil *bitch* all the time?!" John challenged. Dimi started to get out of the car, but Cicci pulled him back into his seat.

"Alright, you know what?" Cicci loudly cut them off, holding up his hands in frustration. "I don't know what yous guys' problem is, but I am sick of this crap! John, get in the back. Dimi, you too."

"What?!" Dimi incredulously asked.

"You heard me," Cicci said. "You two get back there and have it out once and for all." John wasn't sure he'd heard that quite right.

"Sure," Dimi scoffed with a shrug. "I'm game." He climbed out of the front seat and slid into the back in a creepy, weasel-like manner.

"Get back there, too, John," Cicci commanded.

Unsure, John pulled the rear door open and climbed back in. Cicci slid into the driver's seat. He then turned around to face the two disobedient children, each sitting at opposite sides of the seat.

"Dimi, you packin'?" Cicci asked.

"No," Dimi answered like a huffy child.

"John?" Cicci asked, reaching out as he already knew the answer.

John went into his pockets and returned with his .38 Special, handing it over to his boss.

"Any knives?" Cicci checked. "Brass knuckles?" John dug into another pocket and produced a small knife, handing it over as well. Cicci took it before he turned back to the wheel and put the car in gear.

"Alright," Cicci announced. "Ding, ding."

John looked over at Dimi, still unsure of what was happening. Dimi flashed a very malevolent smile at him. John responded with a Roger Moore grin like he was about to face down Jaws on a cable car, but really, it was just to annoy the piss out of Dimi.

Cicci's Ford slowly drove around the Puptown neighborhood. It wasn't that Cicci couldn't drive. It was just he didn't care to when someone else could do it for him. In fact, he was so good a driver, that he was cool as a cucumber as John and Dimi went at it like a pair of vicious dogs in the backseat. He even ignored the groans and audible blows emanating from behind him. His only response was to every so often take a look in the rear view mirror to keep an eye on what was going on.

Dimi had John down on the floorboard, pummeling him with blows. John's mouth had already been bloodied with a split lip. John reached up and gouged his fingers into Dimi's eyes, causing the aggressor to pull away from him with a pained yell.

Cicci's car rounded a corner as John was able to right himself. Cicci whistled nonchalantly to himself. Dimi drew back his arm to throw a punch, but it was caught short and cracked a window with his elbow. As Dimi looked at his arm in confusion, John took the advantage and was suddenly on top of the driver, beating the chump like a dirty Mojave rug. Furious lefts and rights connected as John drove it home with a vengeance. Finally, Dimi slid into the floor, his face all kinds of busted up. Cicci once more looked into the rear view and seeing how the fight had went, he hit the breaks, jerking he and John around and bringing the car to a screeching halt.

"Alright, John, that's enough!" Cicci decreed. John likely didn't hear him though, as he was still bombing away at his helpless opponent.

"John!" Cicci shouted and that time, John heard him because he stopped. "Back off!" the boss ordered and John pulled himself away into the other corner of the back seat. Cicci inspected the damage to his driver and his car from the front seat.

"You clowns better be glad this ain't my Cherry Baby," Cicci alluded to a top-shape cherry-red Corvette he kept in tip-top shape for special occasions.

"Yeah..." John said between sucking in breaths. "You need a sign made for it... *No fighting in the Cherry.*"

"Ain't that the fuckin' truth?" Cicci agreed with a slight grin.

By now, Dimi had finally pulled himself back into the back seat.

"You done?" Cicci asked.

"Yeah, I'm done," Dimi curtly replied, annoyed at the outcome.

"Good," Cicci barked. "Now get your ass back up here and drive me home."

Cicci returned John's weapons to him. Still breathing hard, John put them back into their hiding holes in his coat. Cicci scooted over into his usual passenger's seat. "Outta here, John," he directed.

John glared over at Dimi. "You ever say anything about my future wife again," he warned, "I'll kill ya." John exited the car, slowly followed by Dimi. Cicci rolled down his window as Dimi limped back up into the driver's seat. John poked around at the wounds on his face, a busted lip and numerous bruises.

"You gonna be okay?" Cicci asked with legitimate concern.

"Yeah, fine, Cicci." John replied. "Thanks," he added out of courtesy.

"Alright, I'll see yas later," Cicci said.

"Yo, Fetaccini," Dimi said as he looked up.

"What?" John asked. Cicci rolled his eyes, figuring this wouldn't end well.

"Really," Dimi began, a smile on his bruised face. "Tell Cora I like her hair... when it's bobbin' up an' down my dick!"

Dimi slammed the gas, causing Cicci's tires to squeal. John could only get out an incensed "YOU MOTHER—" before being left behind in a cloud of exhaust.

Cicci turned to Dimi, extremely irritated by his subordinate. "Dimi, that was so uncool," he scolded.

"Hey," Dimi waved him off. "Tough guy can handle it."

John slowly pulled himself up the stairs leading to his apartment. He rolled a shoulder in pain, a pain he was absolutely not going to show Dimi or Cicci. He may have won the fight, but he was still pretty battered.

He made his way over to the apartment door and fished out his keys. He stopped short when he realized the door was unlocked. John opened the door and entered, and almost immediately spotted the refrigerator door open in the kitchen and its light shining out.

"Hey, who's here?" John cautiously queried.

Cora's head popped up from behind the refrigerator door. She was dressed in her Fountainstone servers' garb, her purse draped over her shoulder. She was bent down on one knee raiding the fridge.

"Hey John!" the server cheerily said. "Didn't expect you here."

"That's my line," John replied, leaning against the nearby counter. "Whatcha doin' here, baby?"

"Can you believe it?" Cora asked as she worked. "I forgot to pack a lunch."

"Well if you wouldn't get up so early an' leave so damned fast, you wouldn't forget," John said.

"Oh, I know," Cora admitted, "but I gotta get to work on time. Somebody's gotta pay the bills around here."

John looked away, almost ashamed. Cora meanwhile was completely oblivious as she stood up, food in both hands. For the first time, she got a good look at John's wounded face, which caused her to let out a gasp of shock.

"John, what happened?" she asked with unease. "You look like you caught a Clubber Lang left hook!"

"Someone was say—" he started before cutting himself off. John just looked at Cora. She stared back at him, worry etched all over her face. And he didn't like it. He didn't want to upset this classy, beautiful flower of a woman.

"Nothin'," John lied. "It was nothin'. I'm fine." John bent forward and kissed Cora's forehead. She blinked her eyes and smiled. "Go on. You're gonna be late," he told her. "But don't run. You could trip an' look like me."

Cora started to head off, but turned back once more to John. "You'll be here later, right?" she asked.

"You bet," he replied with a wave.

"I'll see you tonight," Cora said with a smile. She blew John a kiss as she exited the apartment. Her fast footfalls on the stairs outside were like boxes being thrown around quickly.

John slowly sat down on the floor, rather at a loss. "Fuckin' Dimi..." he hissed. He then rested his hand on the floor, but suddenly yanked it away like he'd touched a live electrical wire. "EGGGH!!! Something *is* sticky here!"

Over in the corner of a street's circle in Proton, the lights of a single house that was thumping loud baselines into the 9 o'clock night were still on. The house belonged to Crimilicious and despite his somewhat unsavory character, the house itself was unassuming, as if a middle-class family lived there. It was an off-color white with a porch and windows on the side. You wouldn't look at it twice.

Inside the house, there was a massive party going on with a healthy mix of blacks and Mexicans. The few whites there were mostly young women. The music was even louder than it sounded from the street. Honeys were everywhere as was the booze and the bling. The conversations caused a steady level of roar in addition to the music.

In the back yard, Crimilicious sat behind a round table under the awning of his back porch with Ty and Jerome. They were drinking bottled beer and several empty bottles already littered the top of the table. Partiers would enter or exit the back door every so often, often couples going elsewhere after successfully hooking up.

"I hear Kelson's drinkin's picked up," Jerome stated. "He's been goin' around startin' shit with kids."

"Yeah," Ty concurred. "Heard the other day, he got caught tryin' ta grab itty-bitty-titty."

"Aw, man, that's not right," Crimilicious leaned back with obvious disgust. "Alright, I'll go have a talk with him soon. What about our guy? Heard anything from 'im?"

"He says Cicci's gettin' ready to retire," Jerome informed.

"'Bout time too," Ty retorted. "He's too old. This shit's a young man's game."

"Who's replacin' him?" Crimilicious asked, raising his hands in question.

"Guy says John Fetaccini's the likeliest," Jerome answered.

"Fetaccini?" Crimilicious wondered aloud. "Where have I heard that name before?"

Ty and Jerome looked at each other uncomfortably.

"Um, that thing with your sister," Ty spoke up, clearing his throat. The boss man looked up like he didn't know what he was talking about. "Kim an' that piece a' shit cop," Ty continued. "Fetaccini got pinched beating the living shit out of that guy when he sat on Kim and tried to whale on 'er. He just happened to be wanderin' by and saw it."

The incident finally clicked in Crimilicious' mind. "Ohhh..." he lowly said, slightly nodding. "Yeah, I remember that guy. Respec."

Crimilicious held up his beer bottle. Ty and Jerome followed suit and clinked them together repeating in unison "respec" before downing a mouthful of liquid.

"Fetaccini?" Crimilicious grinned to himself. "Shit, that can't be his real name. Maybe a misspelling?"

"Sheeeet, if it ain't no name," Ty began, "it's a gross misspelling of the word 'fettuccine'."

"You looked in the da mirror lately... *Sean*," Jerome jibed.

"Hey, you think anyone's gonna get any street cred with 'Sean Cassidy,' foo?" Crimilicious defended his cooler street moniker.

An underage teenage boy toppled out the back door, nearly tripping over his feet as he passed across the porch before subsequently loudly vomiting up a night's worth of liquor onto the lawn.

"Yo, man! Can't you find a toilet?!" Crimilicious objected, rising to his feet for emphasis, though it was really just for show. He held up his beer bottle in toast with a grin before laughing.

"Alright, that's enough business for one night," the boss man decreed. "Let's get back to some serious hangin'. There's hos for days in 'ere. Ty, see if our malt liquor's shown up."

"I'm on it like Spencer-for-Fuckin'-Hire, man!" Ty replied before rising to his feet and heading indoors before anyone even knew he was gone.

"And somebody get this pukin' fool off my lawn!" Crimilicious ordered, this time dead serious.

In the bedroom of John and Cora's apartment back in Puptown, Cora lie on top of John as if he were some kind of giant pillow. John's bedclothes were in disarray and the strap of Cora's black bra had slipped down her arm. She grinned like a little girl and her hair was matted to the top of her forehead. They both breathed heavily, Cora a little more so than John. *Rock & Roll Gangsta* played in low volume from the clock radio across the room.

"I do think that *Sex for Dummies* book of yours is payin' off," John observed.

"Right??" Cora agreed. "I feel like I'm vibrating."

"That's just me," John teased.

"Well, vibrate harder," Cora demanded as she went in for an audible smack-y kiss.

"What is that perfume you're wearin'?" John inquired. "How do you smell so great after that? I can feel the sweat on you, honey."

"I don't have any perfume on," Cora admitted. "I showered it off when I got home."

"Well, somethin' on you smells good," John observed. "It's like fresh. A little fruity."

"Is it my shampoo conditioner, maybe?" Cora offered, at a loss. John bent up and took a whiff of Cora's hair.

"And Bingo was his name-o," John said, relaxing back onto the bed. "It's just shampoo?"

"Mm-hmm."

"That you normally buy?"

"Mm-hmm."

"Goddamn, that's some great shampoo conditioner, baby," John declared.

Cora grinned sheepishly as she lay her head onto John's chest.

"I really didn't want to go back to work this afternoon," Cora spoke up.

"Hey, I didn't want you to either," John agreed.

"I'm glad you were here when I got back," Cora continued. "The place is so... empty when you're not here."

"Funny," John began. "I think the same thing when you aren't here."

"Really?" Cora asked.

"Really," John answered.

"Aww..." Cora replied, looking up at John. "I don't know what I'd do without you."

"You'd be fine without me," John surmised.

"I'm scared of everything, John," Cora admitted. "You make me feel safe... like nothing's gonna hurt me as long as you're around."

"Cora, look at me," John said, even though she was already looking at him. "I ain't gonna let nothin' bad happen ta you," he stated with purpose, looking into Cora's eyes as he spoke. "Ever."

"Promise?" Cora asked with a grin that hid back happy tears.

"Promise," John replied.

"Oh..." Cora started to say but never finished as she pulled John in for another kiss.

"Except for..." John began as Cora slowly pulled away. "Here. I'm gonna do ungodly things to you here, woman."

"And what's this?" Cora questioned, feigning innocence as she felt something poke against her thigh. Again. John grabbed Cora and threw her back against the bed as they began to heavily kiss once more.

CHAPTER FIVE -
Every Day I'm Hustlin', Hustlin', Hustlin'…

The West Bar was a local Puptown dive in Klaude, opened by a man with an apparent lack of imagination. It was on the leftmost side of the Puptown section and ergo, the name seemed like a fit. And in case the drunks that frequented it couldn't remember, it actually had a sign hanging over the door announcing itself as *The West Bar*, amongst the usual neon light bar paraphernalia.

John Fetaccini rounded a corner, then entered the modest glass door leading inside. The place was less Cheers and more New York City subway car. Smoke hung over sections of the bar like a thick smog as Gordon Lightfoot's *Sundown* blared over the speakers. The Bartender, an older gentleman in his early fifties, stood proudly behind the bar drying off a washed glass. He eyeballed it, catching sight of John through the bottom.

"Hey John," the Bartender said as he lifted up a finger to point. "There's a guy in the corner askin' for ya."

"Yeah?" John asked rhetorically. "Thanks."

John moved into a booth near a back window to find one Steven Harris sitting alone, nursing a beer. Although it could have been root beer as well, judging by the color. He was about the same age as John, but looked like a fresh-faced teen and was twice as nervous. John walked over to the booth, almost looming over the kid.

"Name's Fetaccini," John began. "You lookin' for me?"

"Yeah... Yeah!" Steven replied. "Glad you could make it. I'm Steven Harris. Cicci says you're a good guy."

John sat down, leaning against the booth and taking off his snap-brim fedora, setting it in the seat beside him.

"I don't know about that," John deprecatingly said. "I hear you gotta job for me. What is it?"

"Cicci suggested I talk to you about this," Steven began. "I came back from Iraq and found things had really gotten bad for my mom, who lives up north." John took out a notepad from his coat and began to scribble into it.

"She didn't tell me about any of this in her letters," Steven continued, "but she missed a payment and the landlord cut off the heat. She tried to pay him, and even slept with him, but he wouldn't put the heat back on."

Steven stopped talking a moment. John could tell he was on the verge of tears, but this was a business meeting. He impassively looked on as Steven recomposed himself. "Now she's caught pneumonia and if she doesn't get well soon, she's gonna die," he eventually got out.

"The name of this landlord?" John asked while writing notes.

"Austin Andrews," the vet said. "He lives on Klinder Street. That's where my mom lives too. The people on the street say Cicci could help me and he pointed me to you. Can you do anything?"

John stopped writing and looked up at Steven. "I heard the words 'a' and 'grand' thrown about. You don't look like you have that much."

"Oh, I do. I do!" Steven reassured. He then began to dig in his pockets. "I've got 1,000 right here."

Steven produced a wad of one grand and handed it to John. The collector inspected it. All green.

"I'm gonna need a little back up for this, just ta be safe," John explained. "Can you get 500 more?"

"Oh sure. Sure!" Steven excitedly said. "By when?"

"How 'bout two weeks?" John mused.

"I'll get it," the boy nodded. "I'll get it for you."

John slid over his notepad to the kid. "Here," he began. "Write down the address of this Andrews and your mom for me."

Steven quickly wrote down the information. "This mean you'll do it?" he asked.

"I'll see what I can do," John said professionally. "You tell your mom there will be heat tonight."

"I'll do that," Steven joyously said. "Thank you so much, Mr. Fetaccini. I'll never forget this."

"Yeah," John skeptically said. "But don't make me come find you in two weeks."

Clemens' car, an old 80s model Monte Carlo, rolled down the road as street kids played on the sidewalk. It was obviously way past the time they should be out. Clemens drove while John rode shotgun. Eagle Eye Cherry's *Save Tonight* played on the radio.

"So I took one of those personality quizzes," Clemens said in the middle of a conversation, "to see what Batman villain I'm most like."

"Batman villain?" John questioned. "What are you, 8?"

"Batman's the shit, John," Clemens defended. "Dude doesn't have any superpowers. Just a couple of dead parents, a belt of gadgets and a hunger for vengeance. I mean, it's the goddamned Batman!"

"Yeah, yeah," John dismissed. "So what's this quiz say?"

"Well," Clemens chuckled. "It said I'd be Catwoman."

"What?!" John asked incredulously before breaking into a fit of laughter.

"Oh, you laugh all you want," Clemens said proudly, "but you know I look good."

"Never knew that's how you were bent, Clemens," John chuckled. "Me? I think I'd be the Scarecrow."

"Scarecrow?" Clemens considered. "That's an interesting choice. Why?"

"Dude rocks a hat," John matter-of-factly said.

"Can't beat that logic," Clemens scoffed

John stretched as he began to yawn. "I don't dig bein' out so late," he said as soon as the yawn would allow. "Already had a long day."

"I hear that," Clemens replied. "But it is what it is. Gotta work for ya bread."

"I think I'd rather just go to the grocery store," John answered. After a moment or two something hit him. "Hey, how was things in Miami?"

"Oh, it was a blast, man," Clemens said enthusiastically. "I met someone!"

"Really?" John inquired. "How was she? Er, that was presumptuous of me. How were 'they'?"

"You're actually right," Clemens proudly deflected the backhanded insult. "'They' ruled. I fell for one of 'em, actually."

"That's great," John legitimately said. "You gonna start goin' out with 'er?'

"How the fuck am I gonna go out with someone in Miami?" Clemens asked.

"I dunno," John shrugged. "Move there? Move her here?"

"I made out with two of them, too," Clemens informed. "Had foreplay with one, and one just fucking about made me blow a load nibbling on my ear."

"Whoa," John said, sounding especially Butt-Head-esque. "Blondes, I s'pose?"

"No, actually," Clemens corrected. "Brunettes."

"Alright, my man!" John cheered as the two high-fived. "That's what I'm talkin' about!"

"The one I fell for," Clemens continued, "she doesn't know I like her."

"Jesus, Clemens," John chided. "Why didn't you tell 'er?!"

"No guts," Clemens admitted.

"No guts, no vadge," John explained. "Law of the jungle, Clem."

"I know," Clemens agreed. "I'm going to tell 'er hopefully. She gave me her address and number because she wants prints of the photos I took of us together."

"You'll have to show me sometime," John said.

"So we'll have to see if I go see her again," Clemens mused.

"Go! You got to," John urged.

"We'll see," Clemens waved him off.

"That's great, Clemens," John sarcastically replied. "'Definitely... maybe... perhaps'..."

Ricky Martin's *La Vida Loca* suddenly came on the radio, much to the chagrin of John whose face visibly reacted to the sound.

"Get this crap off the radio, Clemens!" John said with palpable disgust.

"Hey, John," Clemens balked. "You know the rules of the road."

"Actually... I don't," John admitted.

"Driver picks the music. Passenger shuts his piehole about it," Clemens informed. "Besides, you can't be badmouthin' the Mexican anthem like that."

"Wait, what?!" John incredulously asked.

"You heard me," Clemens retorted.

"Ugh," John groaned. "I remember when this was new. I said 'Forget loca, I'll be in a goddamned rubber room if this piece a' shit is still on the radio in six months'."

"I remember," Clemens nodded. "Back when you thought everybody on the radio was Creed."

"Ooh," John considered. "Creed... the Nickelback of the 90's. How naive we all were..."

"Hey, John," Clemens spoke up.

"Yeah?" the collector replied.

"Do you know how you go to a Creed concert?" the driver queried.

"With earplugs?" John shot back.

"No."

"Then how?" John asked, not seeing he was being set up.

"With ahms wide oh-puhn," Clemens sang in the cadence of Creed's lead singer. He and John suddenly broke into a fit of laughter, despite themselves.

"Seriously, though," John began, "you should take earplugs to any concert you go to. That shit's *loud* and you could go deaf."

Clemens looked over at John like that was the weirdest thing he'd heard in a while.

It was a cold, windy night with a crescent moon high in the sky. In fact, one might expect to see the Dark Knight jumping around about the bricked rooftops of the buildings in the area. But there was a different sort of vigilantism being dished out tonight.

Austin Andrews was thrown against an exitway wall with a thud. He was a rough-looking guy dressed in a sweater. Slightly balding with a mustache. He looked like someone mothers warned their kids about. John and Clemens stood nearby. Clemens shook his hand in pain.

"Clemens, you don't punch right," John observed. "Ya gotta hit with yer knuckles, not yer fingers."

"Yeah, yeah," Clemens replied. "When do we get ta danglin' him over the side of the roof dere?"

"Plan A never works out," John surmised. "Let's just beat the hell out of 'im an' get it over with."

Andrews coughed as he wiped blood away from his mouth. "What do you assholes want, anyway?" he barked.

"Ms. Harris over in 490 ain't got no heat," John explained. "She's got pneumonia. You don't turn on the heat, she'll die."

"Hey, that ain't my problem," Andrews replied. "She didn't pay on time."

"She fucked your brains out so you'd turn the heat on, you jackass!" John angrily shot back. He didn't like it when some jerk took advantage of someone else like this.

"Yeah," Andrews chuckled. "And she wasn't even that good a lay."

John hauled off and punched Andrews flush on the chin, crumpling him to the ground. He then stepped toward the groaning man, brandishing his knife.

"Here's what yer gonna do," John began. "You're gonna turn that woman's heat on *tonight*. Or I'm gonna come back here and cut off a finger. Dealer's choice."

He then grabbed Andrew's chin and pushed it up to make him look into his eyes to drive the point home. "And if you still don't do it, I'm gonna call up some hard-hittin' mo-fos. Pipes and such, dig? Do the right thing for once, jackhole."

John then shoved Andrews to the ground. He turned and headed away, back to Clemens, beckoning him with a "come on." As John and Clemens disappeared within the exit stairwell back into the building, Andrew wiped his mouth again, wondering aloud what the hell a "jackhole" was.

John alone walked to the door of apartment 490 and knocked. After a few moments, the door began to open. Creakingly slow. The tenant, Ms. Harris, a sickly-looking middle-aged woman stood there, timidly peering out from behind the door.

"Yes?" the lady barely audibly asked.

"Ms. Harris? That's you, right?" John asked.

"Yes..." Ms. Harris unsurely said. "Who are you?"

"That's not important," John deflected. "What is important is I wanted to let you know your heat will be on tonight."

"Wha... ?" Ms. Harris incredulously asked. John dug into his coat and handed over a sheet of paper to the woman.

"And if it doesn't," John continued, "then you send someone here and let me know, okay?"

Ms. Harris looked over the paper through her glasses.

"Now you rest up and get better," John recommended. "We don't need you dyin' on Steven, right?"

Almost as fast as he appeared, John turned and left, leaving Ms. Harris confused, but happy.

"Why... thank you!" she could barely get out.

Clemens' old car made its way down the lonely Klaude streets. This time, John drove and was quite good at it for someone that didn't have a car. Clemens was busy counting Steven Harris' money. He counted off 500 big boys then gave the remainder to John, who quickly pocketed his remaining grand.

"We got out of there nice and early," Clemens said. "It's only 9:30."

"Eh, I still hate late jobs, though," John huffed. "Hey, thanks for the ride, Clemens."

"No problem, John," Clemens said. "But you really need to get a car."

"Oh, no problem," John replied. "Just let me call my broker, E.F. Nuttin."

"John, I'm a bit sleepy," Clemens said ignoring him. "Can you handle things?"

"No worries," John assured.

"You sure?" Clemens asked for clarification. "You're not sleepy or anything?"

"I'm fine," the collector said slightly annoyed.

"I'm serious," Clemens pushed. "I'm gonna take a nap. Don't fall asleep."

"Clemens, I'm not gonna fall asleep drivin' the fuckin' car!" John snapped.

"Okay, John," Clemens yawned. "But you realize that if you do fall asleep, in the obituary, it's gonna say 'Also killed was John Fetaccini'?"

Clemens curled into a nap position as John glared at him from the corner of his eye before turning his attention back to the road.

Back in John's old neighborhood, Clemens car pulled around and stopped. The doors opened and both men got out. Clemens walked around to the driver's side and re-entered the car.

"Thanks for the lift," John said.

"Anytime," Clemens replied. "See ya tomorrow."

"Yeah," the collector automatically said.

The Monte Carlo pulled away, leaving John alone on the streets other than the streetlights blazing down on him every so often. John walked a few feet then noticed a shiny object. It was a small, golden necklace with a large heart pendant. John picked it up and clocked the area for any possible owners. He then opened it, finding nothing inside. No picture, no inscription, nothing. Without a second though, John pocketed it and moved on.

Cora sat in her chair, alone in their apartment, reading a book entitled *Stressed? Slow Down Before You Hurt Someone.* The door rattled and then opened and John came into the room, pulling Cora away from her reading.

"When'd you get home?" John asked, shutting the door and locking it behind himself.

"Oh, about 8:15," Cora said. "Where were you?"

"On a job," he rather vaguely replied.

Cora put down her book. "John, you didn't... ?"

"Not today, sweetie," John answered as if she'd asked if he picked up any milk. "Uh, tomorrow night, I was thinkin' that maybe we should go out together and do somethin' fun. Would you like that?"

"I'd like that," Cora smiled. "I like going out with you."

"Yeah?" John replied. "Well I like goin' out with you."

John walked around behind Cora's chair and blindfolded her with his fingers.

"Uh, what are you doing, John?" Cora asked, unsure of what was happening.

"Guess what I got," John said in an almost sing-song voice.

"It better not be herpes," Cora coldly said.

"Uh... no," John equally coldly replied.

"Then what?" she questioned.

John pulled out the necklace he pocketed and dangled it in front of Cora's eyes before releasing his hand from her head. "Ta-da!" he merrily said.

Cora gasped. "For me??"

"Of course," the collector clarified.

John dropped the necklace into Cora's palm. Cora looked up and gave John a long, passionate kiss that threatened to suck his head into her mouth.

Suddenly, there was a fast, hard knock on the door. Cora broke away, disappointedly. John sighed, before heading over to the door and opening it. Cicci stood before him.

"'Ey, Cicci," John respectfully greeted.

"Listen, John," Cicci began. "We need your help, pronto."

"Did Geno's cat get stuck in that tree again?" John legitimately queried. "I told you guys to buy a ladder from—"

"There's these guys over at this bar that're a little behind on some payments," Cicci said, ignoring him. "So me and Dimi and Vinelli are goin' over to collect. We kinda need you, John."

"Well..." John unsurely said. He turned looking longingly back to Cora. He wanted to help his boss, but more he wanted to stay in with his girl.

"Go on, John," Cora said, resigning herself to the inevitable.

John turned back to his boss. "Let's drive, baby," he declared.

Cicci turned to leave and John followed out the door behind him. Left behind in the apartment alone again, Cora sighed to herself.

"Just when it's getting good," Cora began, "it's always 'this guy owes me money', 'help us get this cat out of that tree', 'where's that goddamned generator'?" She sadly looked down at her chest. "Looks like it's another night in with the girls..."

Cora put her book onto the nearby table and stood up. Her scrunched-up clothes were pulled down by gravity. She looked forlornly at the front door.

"Someday we won't have to worry about work and bills and all this other crap," Cora reflected. "It'll just be you and I, John... Right?"

The front door offered no answers.

"Right?" Cora weakly asked again.

Cicci's Ford sat idling on the street near John's apartment complex. A bruised and bandaged Dimi sat in the driver's seat. John and Cicci appeared from an entry way. John opened the door for Cicci, and followed him into the back seat. Inside was a younger Italian man by the name of Vinelli. He was regular-sized and with blondish hair, a tell-tale sign of originating from northern Italy.

"Hey, Vinelli," John greeted as he caught sight of him.

"How's it goin', John?" the pleasant fellow asked.

"Same ol' shit, different day," John remarked. "You feelin' better now?"

"Like a million ducks," Vinelli said.

"Um, I think that's 'a million bucks'," John corrected.

"Yeah," Vinelli admitted, "but think about it: a million ducks have to feel pretty good too!"

"Listen, John," Cicci said, growing weary of these shenanigans. "I don't want no trouble with these guys unless we have to, so kindly keep your mouth shut. We just need you with us in case they try something."

"Got it, Cicci," John answered obediently.

The door of a small-time bar opened and Cicci entered, followed by John, Dimi, and Vinelli. The whole place was filled with degenerate drunks, many of whom were passed out over the bar or on tables. The more sober of the bunch played games of pool in the back side of the room. A burly bartender stood near a cash register, going over the day's earnings. As the four collectors advanced, he looked up.

"Can we help you?" the bartender plainly asked.

"We need to see Marty," Cicci informed.

"In back," the bartender pointed.

The four hoodlums walked off towards the back room. Noting the cash, John turned around and went back to the bartender.

"Help Jerry's Kids?" John coolly asked.

"John!" Cicci lowly shouted from the back. John turned around and followed his boss properly, leaving the bartender rather dumbfounded by the whole thing.

"Jerry's Kids??" the bartender asked to himself aloud. "Who the hell's Jerry?!"

Marty Manfield moved some large boxes containing booze about in the back room. He was a short, young black man with an unlikely head of blonde hair. On his wrist was a glaringly garish "gold" watch that was most likely painted as such. The door of the room opened, revealing Cicci and the others, who entered, and crowded the area up badly.

"Cicci," Marty said as he looked behind himself. "What are you doin' here this late?"

"My man, Marty!" Cicci cheerily said. "How's business goin'?"

"It's pretty good," Marty replied. "You can see lots of people like to get shitfaced when the workin' day's done."

John moved as best he could about the room, studying something on his notepad. The others, though, stood still behind their boss.

"Did you happen to catch the game?" Cicci asked, doing his best to curtail the conversation.

"What game?" Marty responded, pushing a box into a stack over his head.

"Green Bay and Dallas?" Cicci answered with a question.

"No," Marty nervously said. "I missed it." He obviously did not.

"Well, I happened to catch it," Cicci informed. "It—"

"Come outside with me," Marty interrupted. "Let's get some fresh air."

"Well..." Cicci sputtered, "Okay."

Marty exited the room followed by the others. The fresh air they got was more of a haze of cigarette smoke. An attractive girl in a pair of jean shorts three sizes too small leaned over a jukebox near the back room, reading the songs available. Marty lead the collectors over to the cash register with John slowly bringing up the rear. A dance mix of Elton John's *Saturday Night's Alright for Fighting* improbably began to play over the bar's speakers. Even more, the girl that chose it equally improbably began to dance in earnest to it.

Marty grabbed a bottle of champagne and turned back to his visitors. "Hey Johnny," he said getting the collector's attention. John hated being called "Johnny" by people that weren't close to him. "Where'd you get that hat?"

"You like it?" John asked, tipping the brim. "Cora gave it to me. She's got good taste, don'tcha think?"

"Yeah, I like it," Marty lied. "But you look like you belong on a Panama Jack t-shirt."

The others politely giggled, even if it was a backhanded compliment.

"Where'd you get that watch?" John queried.

"This is a 250-dollar watch, John," Marty said, looking over his wrist. "You like it?"

"Yeah, I like it," John also lied, "but you look like you should be bitch-slapping girls in fishnets." John punctuated it with a smart-ass grin that was bound for trouble.

"Listen, Marty, about the game..." Cicci tried to regain control of the conversation.

"Could ya turn the music down?" John interrupted. "It's gettin' on my nerves. Who the hell does a dance remix of *Saturday Night's Alright for Fightin'* anyway?"

"John," Cicci warned.

"The girls like it," Marty responded, pointing to the dancing girl in the distance.

"You call that a girl?" John stated more than asked. "That's a slut, that's what that is. There aren't any girls anywhere in here. Real girls'd be embarrassed to be caught dead here."

"John, shut up," Cicci said, losing patience. "Marty, listen..."

"That's it," Marty decreed. "I'm not payin'."

"Whoa, whoa, Marty!" Cicci said with a smile and a shrug. "Did I say anything about money?"

"Doesn't matter, cause I'm not payin'," Marty barked.

"You better fuckin' pay!" John said, punctuated by pointing his index finger at the young man.

"I don't pay poseurs," Marty matter-of-factly said.

Groans erupted from the collectors, followed by an almost never-ending parade of "'ey"s and "whoa"s. John Fetaccini started looking around the immediate area, likely for any possible potential weapons.

"Marty, Marty," Cicci said. "Calm down, man! I just came to ask you if you saw the game and now you're gettin' fuckin' fresh callin' me and my friends poseurs?" He looked back to his men. "The balls on this kid!"

"I'll show ya 'kid'!" Marty snarled before throwing a right punch that hit Cicci flush in the face.

Immediately everybody in the place that wasn't inhibited by liquor—and even a few who were—ran over to the group. John was in the middle of it all, grabbing a hold of Marty and pounding an alternating series of punches into his unfortunate face.

The entire bar was fighting, but the Italians were holding their ground, most of them now kicking Marty on the ground. The girl in the tight shorts drank from a beer bottle safely tucked in a nook, watching the whole ordeal. "Kick their ass!" she shouted to no one in particular.

Elsewhere, Dimi and a barfly were going at it, stupidly standing toe-to-toe exchanging blows. Another barfly grabbed Vinelli and threw him onto an arcade game.

Meanwhile in Cora's bathroom, she sat reclined in the bathtub, covered up to her biceps in bubbles. The room was lit by candlelight and the air was permeated by the relaxing sounds of Enya's *Wild Child*. Whether Cora was asleep or not was indecipherable, but she was very, very relaxed. Possibly much more than the atmosphere itself. All that was missing was her man.

Back at the bar, a cacophony of chaos ruled the night. Dimi threw the barfly he was fighting onto the ground with a very sloppy judo slam.

John grabbed hold of the barfly that was manhandling Vinelli and threw two rights then a left hook that knocked him spiraling to the ground. For good measure, he then kicked the downed man several times in the side. Calming down, John started to look around seeing the entirety of the fight. Having had enough, he whipped out his .38 Special and shot into the air. Dust and pieces of the ceiling fell down on him, mostly hitting his hat's brim. Everyone almost en masse stopped what they were doing and looked over at him.

"Gentlemen, do I have your attention?" John asked as if he had some moral authority. "We're here for Marty's money an' we're not leavin' till we get it. Anyone don't wanna get hurt best ease off. Anyone does wanna get hurt better think twice an' ease on out the back."

The combatants started to back away from each other.

"Marty, give us some money," John demanded.

Marty was busted up pretty badly and bleeding from the mouth. Even his fake blonde hair was stained with blood. Nevertheless, he still had the energy to get himself over to the cash register. He pulled out three hundred dollars and begrudgingly paid off Cicci. Cicci took the money then turned and left. Vinelli and Dimi soon followed. John continued to stand there with his pistol keeping the place in check. It seemed as if he might have something to say but instead, he suddenly turned and darted out the bar.

Cicci's car outside peeled out and sped off into the night as soon as everybody was inside. Well, mostly, anyway; Vinelli's leg was still hanging out when the car started moving. Inside, John removed his hat and dusted the debris off into the floor.

"John, what the hell's the matter with you?!" Cicci demanded to know.

"What's the matter with me?" John replied in legitimate shock. "What's the matter with them?!"

"We coulda just been in an' out if we played it cool," Cicci explained, "but you had to shoot your mouth off, not to mention your damned gun! What if some jag-bag called the cops, then what?!"

"Hey, hey," John began. "Okay, maybe it got a little extreme."

"Ya think?!" Cicci interrupted.

"But I ain't gonna let nobody talk to you like that punk did," John continued. "He's lucky he's still in one piece." John turned to look out the rear window. "In fact, later tonight—"

"You'll do no such thing, John!" Cicci cut him off and drove it home pointing in John's face. "And that's an order."

Vinelli rubbed a bruise on his face. He obviously wasn't used to this sort of thing. "I shoulda stayed sick," he groaned.

A small lamp lit up the room in John's apartment revealing very little of the place. Cora was sound asleep in her bathrobe on the couch. The TV was playing an infomercial but was barely audible. The door to John's apartment opened and he entered, locking the door behind himself. He noted Cora on the couch and made a beeline for her. He turned the television off before carefully hauling her into his grasp.

John opened the bedroom door with his legs and entered with the still-asleep Cora in tow. He walked over to their bed and gently laid Cora onto it. He then walked back over to the door, closed it, took off his hat, and tossed it onto Cora's table.

"I was waiting for you," Cora drowsily said.

"You shoulda just went to bed," John told her as he stepped out of his boots.

"Then I wouldn't have got ta see you," she explained.

"Your eyes are shut, baby," John said as he climbed into the bed beside her. "You can't see me."

"Always with the details, John," Cora mumbled. John bent over and kissed his girl's forehead, resulting in a peaceful smile from her as she drifted back off to sleep.

CHAPTER SIX -
Rule #1: You Don't Talk About Date Night

The next morning, Sarrageno and Vinelli were hard at work scrubbing the walls outside the Puptown Gentlemen's Club. Disparaging graffiti had been tagged onto the walls from the previous night. *These guys suck dick!*, *Fetaccini's mom fucks bums in hell*, and *Colone was in on 9-11!* populated the concrete walls.

Sarrageno looked over at his colleague. "What the fuck did you guys do last night?!" he asked, more than a little annoyed. Vinelli just shrugged.

Inside, Cicci sat at his table looking extremely unhappy and impatient. John sat next to him looking equally impatient. Sitting across from them was Lins Tacket, a bespectacled, short man who looked like he was more nervous than he'd ever been in his life.

"They just shitcanned me for no reason," Lins said uneasily. "Not even any severance pay. I don't have money for food or lovin'. Damned republicans in office won't help me."

"And you want a loan to bang some masseuse?" Cicci inquired skeptically.

"I-I love her!" Lins chattered.

Cicci looked over to John who seemed to be giving some sort of psychic double facepalm, as his arms weren't even above the table.

"Misty and I share true love!" Lins injected.

"Uh, right..." Cicci patronized.

"We can only meet at the parlor," Lins began, less nervous than before. "And I don't have her cell phone number. But our love for one another is true!"

"Well, now..." Cicci seemed to consider.

"You only see her at some 'massage parlor' and you still don't have her phone number?" John spoke up. It was obvious by his tone that he'd listened to enough of this.

"Hey, John..." Cicci tried to interrupt, but John sprang to his feet, ignoring him.

"That's your idea of true love?!" John asked as if he actually wanted an answer. "You wouldn't know true love if it gave you a goddamned reach-around!"

Cicci dropped his forehead into the palm of his hand and ran it through his hair. "John, sit down and calm down before you fall down," he grumbled. John audibly growled at Lens before slowly sitting back down.

"We'll..." Cicci began, looking over at John. "We'll take it under advisement."

"Oh, thank you, Cicci!" Lins said, his face lit up with relief. "Thank you! You don't know how much I need this."

Lins stood up and turned away to exit. As he left, he was almost skipping away with joy. John watched partway in surprise, partway in disgust.

"Where do these people come from, John?" Cicci huffed in frustration. "I'm not giving that weirdo a loan. Even if you kick the crap out of him, he's probably still not gonna have it."

Cicci chomped down on a stogie and lit it up to relax. "Has anybody found the rest of my stogies?!" he questioned to no one in particular. "I'm on my last one here!"

"Still lookin', Cicci!" Vinelli shouted back from nearby. Cicci grimaced and rolled his eyes in frustration.

Cora Secillia chewed on a banana during her lunch hour as she walked down a sidewalk in a busy shopping center in Puptown, her purse in tow around her shoulder. People milled about to and fro all around her. Cora passed several shops as she walked and ate, not so much window-shopping as window browsing. However, one particular shop grabbed her attention and she came to a slow stop, peering into the window. It was a wedding store with everything one might need to get married. Dresses, tuxes, flower arrangements. The works.

From outside, Cora could see a beautiful paper-white wedding dress mounted onto a mannequin. Behind it was a clerk and an engaged couple excitedly going over what must have been their wedding plans. Cora smiled as she looked in, watching them.

But then, suddenly, all that faded away. It wasn't some strange couple in the store. It was Cora the clerk was attending to. She was garbed in the wedding dress she saw, spinning around and showing it off. John was there, looking up at her and watching with approval. The clerk also seemed to approve. Fantasy Cora was having the happiest day of her life.

"Hey, baby!" some stranger nearby said.

Suddenly, Cora snapped back to reality. She was still outside the wedding store, still chewing on her banana. She might have only gone away a little while, but it felt like forever and a day to her.

"If you're lookin' for somethin' ta put in your mouth..." the voice continued.

Cora looked around, rudely awakened from her daydream with daggers shooting from her eyes. Over her shoulder, she found a male teenage boy standing nearby with a lecherous, though legitimately inquisitive look on his face as if he actually expected positive results.

"Really?" Cora asked, hardly able to hide her aggravation. "That's your move? I was havin' a moment here," she gestured at the shop's window, "and you ruin it with *that*? With moves like that, you will be throttling your cock for the rest of your life, sir."

"Whoa, whoa..." the boy said defensively. "Didn't know you were on the rag. Sor-*ree*."

The young perv turned to walk off, thinking he'd told Cora what's what. Cora groaned with frustration then drew back and hucked what was left of her banana at him. The teenager turned back to her in annoyance.

"Hey, bitch! Watch it!" he shouted.

Cora just charged away in the opposite direction in frustration. Moments later, a young blonde girl in her early 20s nearly careened into her. The girl grabbed Cora by the shoulders.

"Hug me, please," the blonde pleaded.

"Wha??" Cora asked, still jostled.

"Please hug me like you haven't seen me in forever!" the blonde girl explained. "My ex is after me and he's right—"

Cora cut her off, wrapping her arms around the girl and pulling her into an embrace. "Where have you been all this time??" she questioned as if the blonde had been a childhood friend. A legitimately warm grin crept across the blonde girl's face.

Nearby, the girl's ex emerged. He was a little older than she was, light brown hair and visibly exuding an air of collegate bro. He stopped himself when he saw that his quarry and Cora were up ahead still embraced. He huffed and then hissed out a "fuck" before turning and heading away in defeat.

Cora pulled back and put an arm around the blonde. "Come on," she spoke up.

The two women turned and wandered off. The blonde put her own arm around Cora.

"What's your name?" Cora inquired.

"Su... Suzy," the blonde hesitantly replied.

"Nice to meet you, Suzy," Cora warmly told her in an attempt to convince her she was safe. "I'm Cora," she continued as they wandered the opposite way down the sidewalk. "Ever heard of Fountainstone... ?"

That night at the West Bar, John sat on a stool with Sarrageno to his immediate right, swigging down a bottle of Dos Equis beer. Sarrageno was chatting up a young, attractive Italian girl who was probably jailbait. The Bartender worked nearby cleaning glasses and beer mugs.

A television showing the day's sports scores played in the background. The place was fairly busy, probably about 75% full.

"Wanna get lucky tonight?" Geno inquired to his young ladyfriend, who simpered and twisted away in a flirty manner.

"No thanks, baby," John retorted as he took another sip of beer. Geno turned and lightly smacked John in the back of his head.

"Not you, ya guinea numbskull!" Geno balked. John just chuckled to himself and took another drink.

The very unhappy-looking Randall Fryers entered the joint, noticed by absolutely no one. He clocked the room and found John at the bar before starting in that direction. In his left hand, he hid a switchblade.

"Kids, I gotta run," John announced. "Date night awaits."

"See ya, John," Sarrageno replied. "Take it easy, man."

"Nice meeting you," Geno's Italian galpal offered up.

John finished the Dos Equis bottle, then got up from the stool and bumped into Fryers. Fryers became even more incensed than he already was. John didn't even recognize him.

"Whoops," John good-naturedly reacted. "Sorry, guy."

John's eyes cut down and spied the switchblade. Fryers immediately tried to stab him with a telegraphed motion but John weaved out of the way, grabbed the assailant's arm, and hit his wrist causing the knife to clink to the floor.

The bar patrons started to take notice. Fryers swung his other arm for a sloppy punch. John ducked and countered with a right to the gut and a left hook to the jaw that sent Fryers sprawling to the floor, knocked completely out for the night. The patrons broke out into cheers and applause. John put up his hands with a slight smile to acknowledge their response.

"Who's tryin' ta kill you this time, John?" the bartender belted out from behind the bar.

"Before tonight, I thought it was just the electric company," John quipped. He bent down to the unconscious Fryers and got a look at him, using a hand to better see the body's face.

"I know who this bastard is," John reported. "It's fuckin' Fryers. Had to collect from him a few days ago and he wouldn't pay up. Probably thought he could get his money back or something. Hell, I dunno."

"You okay, John?" Sarrageno asked, now standing next to him.

"What? Oh, that was nothin'," John replied. "Throw this guy out in a dumpster or somethin', will ya? Fuckin' told you, Fryers—you suffer from a bad case a' slow."

John strode off for the exit, leaving Fryers behind to sleep it off on the bar floor.

It was an unusually calm night at John's apartment complex, no bickering couples or police sirens to offend the ear. Just a dark sky and a brisk wind.

John made his way down the sidewalk that led to his complex. He opened the door to the stairway to his upstairs apartment but stopped short to find Cora sitting on the steps, apparently waiting for him. She wore a thin, sleeveless, deep blue and white dress with a splattery pattern scheme and tan, open-toed sandals.

"Cora, what're you doin' out here?" John asked with concern.

"Why don't you check the door?" Cora responded, hitching her thumb up the stairs.

John angrily ran up the stairs as best he could and spied a note attached to the door of their apartment. Scrawled on the note in poor handwriting was:

"Absolutely no entry inside for three hours while bug bomb goes off. 7:12— Management."

"Son of a *bitch*!" John growled. He turned and slowly went back down the stairs and sat beside Cora.

"Yeah..." she mumbled.

"We don't even have bugs!" John protested as if it made a difference.

"I know, right?" Cora agreed.

"That damned handyman just doesn't like me," John said as he turned and looked back at door. "Of all the dumb, fuckin' luck! I guess that kills our night out."

"Technically, we are out together, John," Cora pointed out.

"Date night sucks tonight," John smirked.

"Amen," Cora sighed.

John noticed the goose bumps on Cora's arms indicating she was cold. "Here," he said to get her attention. John took off his overcoat and wrapped it around Cora.

"Thank you," she cooed as she buried herself within it like a burrito.

"Come on," John said, looking around. "Let's take a stroll."

The two stood up and headed for the downstairs exit before wandering off into the Klaude night. Cora involuntarily pulled John in closer with an arm as they started down the stairs.

A nearby Laundromat was still open, its neon yellow lighting spilling out the windows into the parking lot. The place was filled with the noise of washers and driers doing the neighborhood's clothes as well as a television playing the night's *Wheel of Fortune*. Behind a counter was a late-middle-aged Korean man watching, playing along and using the show to better his English.

John and Cora sat in customer chairs, leaning against one another. Cora was still wrapped in John's overcoat.

"She should've been a model," John said, apparently in the middle of a conversation. "I mean, they gave her way too much credit when they had her sign acting contracts."

"Wait, she's an actress?" Cora asked. "I always thought Megan Fox was an animatronic prop, like those dinosaurs in *Jurassic Park*?"

John chuckled. The resulting break in conversation quickly became somewhat awkward.

"Yep," Cora sighed. "Date night is definitely a bust."

"We don't even have any bread to go feed ducks in the park," John mused.

"We don't even have any ducks in the park," Cora pointed out.

"Touché, smartie-hottie," John permitted.

Cora let out another sigh.

"What's wrong?" John asked.

"Is this what you thought your life would be like?" Cora replied.

"This is a little better, actually..." John answered.

"Yeah?" Cora asked in surprise. "I thought I'd be doing better than this by now."

"Doin' better how?" John inquired. "Doin' what?"

"I'm ring carding again this weekend," Cora began. "You know what I think about that. It just makes me feel like I'm not good enough to do anything else. Like all I can do is be a piece of meat for cretins that can't keep count on their own."

"I don't see why you do it if it makes you so unhappy," John said, running his fingers through her hair.

"Gotta eat," Cora bluntly replied. "I've been looking around. I'm not qualified to do anything."

"If I paid you, would you sing *It's Raining Men?*" John joked, trying to cheer her up.

"No," Cora said with a sigh. But then she thought about it for a moment. "How much?" she queried listlessly.

"Twen'y bucks," John answered.

Cora suddenly got up, throwing John's coat from her back like she was beginning a dramatic dance number in a musical. She immediately began to dance about the place.

"It's rainin' men! Hallelujah, it's rainin' men!" Cora sang. "I'm gonna go out to run and let myself get absolutely soaking wet! It's rainin' men! Hallelujah, it's rainin' men! Every specimen! Tall, blonde, dark and lean. Rough and tough and strong and mean!"

John whipped out a cigarette lighter and flicked on the flame, though why he had one was anyone's guess as he didn't smoke. Cora suddenly stopped.

"Why'd ya stop?" John whined. "I was likin' that."

"Where's my twenty?" Cora demanded, a hand stretched out.

The Korean proprietor angrily marched over to the two. "This look like Karaoke bar?!" he angrily asked before pointing at the door. "Wash something or get out!"

With no clothes to clean at the Laundromat, John and Cora vacated the premises. They wandered about the area of their neighborhood, not venturing away too far. John explained his less-than-interesting day not collecting. Cora told John about the girl she met and how she'd taken her back to the Fountainstone Lodge and called her a cab to take her home.

Some hours later, John and Cora were finally able to get back to their apartment. They had decided to try and salvage Date Night with a board game. They sat across from one another at the dinner table in the kitchen, a Monopoly board sprawled out between them. However, instead of the normal pieces, John had a small monster figurine and Cora had a little Hello Kitty that seemed like a monster in comparison to the hotel game pieces.

A radio played soft music in the background. At the moment, Spandau Ballet was pontificating about what was *True*. A scented candle flickered nearby as John and Cora went through the motions of playing the game.

"I can still smell the bomb," Cora said with a sharp inhale. "Can you?"

"Not as bad as I could," John said, not looking up from the board.

"You hear they're coming out with another *Saw* movie?" Cora asked as she rolled the dice.

"Another?!" John incredulously asked.

"This one's just being called *Jigsaw*, because... reasons?" Cora announced with a shrug.

"Those movies ran out of plot after like the first one and they just kept making 'em," John grumbled. "Is that what people think is a good horror movie now?"

"I guess so," Cora unsurely replied as she moved her Kitty. "Sad isn't it?"

"I blame the Germans," John stated.

"The Germans?" Cora asked, taken aback. "The hell do they have to do with it? Well, besides the obvious?"

"Yeah," John explained. "Back in the 70s, the Germans made this movie that was the first of its kind called *Mark of the Devil* and it had the guy from the *Pink Panther* movies... you know, Clouseau's boss."

"Dreyfus?" Cora answered. "I love the *Pink Panthers*! Well, the ones with Peter Sellers anyway."

"Dreyfus, yeah," John clarified. "What he was doing in it, I'll never know."

"Booze money," Cora matter-of-factly said as she looked at the back of a Chance card.

"But this movie *Mark of the Devil* was the very first torture-porn kind of film because all they did the whole movie was torture women ta death," John continued. "It's even got like an eyeball's point of view shot as one is poked out. Like what you would see momentarily before you went blind?"

"Ugh!" Cora said with a shiver. "That's disgusting."

"It was!" John agreed. "And this movie was really successful. And get this—the Germans cut it up in their version of the movie, but it's actually gorier in our American version. And then they made a sequel and it was successful too and so all of these movies that came out in this time period tried to hop on the bandwagon. But back then, it fizzled out really fast 'cause I guess people got tired of it. I think the only real American movie that got in on it was *Texas Chainsaw Massacre*. But then decades later, shit like *Saw* and *Hostel* came around and brought it back and it hasn't gone away since."

"I hated *Texas Chainsaw Massacre*," Cora offered.

"Why?" John wondered aloud.

"Cause it's not a film," Cora explained. "It's like watching somebody's demented home movie."

"It's not very professional-looking, no," John agreed as he moved his monster to destroy B&O Railroad.

"And the last half hour, my God!" Cora said with protest. "It's nothing but screaming and noise. It was just so annoying to watch." Cora punctuated it with a shudder.

"What's your idea of a good, scary movie, Cora?" John asked.

"Gimme a minute," Cora said as she looked over the board. "I can't think about scary movies and game board finance at the same time."

"That's probably how Wall Street fucked everything up," John grinned.

"I wouldn't doubt it," Cora laughed. She rolled and moved her Hello Kitty the appropriate spaces. "There's so many. *Halloween, A Nightmare on Elm Street.* The originals, of course. Not those awful remakes. *Scream...* well, no, *Scream* was more fun than scary. *The Entity* scared the shit out of me when I was a girl."

"*The Entity*, that's interesting," John admitted. "That was supposed to be based on a true story."

"I KNOW!" Cora loudly said, widening her eyes. "That's what made it so fucked up! What about you?"

"There was this movie Christopher Lee made back in the 60s called *The Devil's Bride*," John said, rolling the dice.

"Mmm," Cora thought. "I don't think I know that one. Christopher Lee... he's the Dracula guy right?"

"I wouldn't let him hear you say that," John chided. "You might know him better as Saruman or Count Dooku."

"Oh, yes, yes," Cora said.

"I saw it on TV when I was 10 or 11 and it scared the *hell* out of me," John began. "Here's how bad the bad guys are: Lee is the *hero* in this. There's this satanist, I forget his name. Anyway, he's trying to steal away, like, Lee's nephew or something and this young girl to turn them over to the devil. The satanist uses black magic to attack and Lee uses white magic to defend and it's actually really mature in its usage of magic and witchcraft."

"Sounds... magical," Cora chortled.

"Eh, not really," John balked. "It's pretty intense a lot of the time, if I remember. But that's not what's important. The important part is how the movie was made. It was leisurely without being slow and it built up suspense and dread and made you nervous the whole movie. Especially when the devil actually showed up. That shit was creepy as fuck. I made the mistake of watching it with the lights off. Never again, baby."

"See, that's something horror movies are missing today: suspense," Cora offered up. "They traded 'em in for jump scares, which aren't so much scary as annoying. It's pathetic that something made in, like, the 30s can be scarier than what they put out today."

"Pretty lame, Milhouse," John nodded.

"*I Walked With a Zombie* freaked me the hell out when we saw it that one Halloween," Cora admitted. "And what was that? 1940?"

"We need more *I Walked With a Zombie*s and less *Saw*s," John postulated.

"I could do with less *I Walked With a Zombie*s," Cora countered. She moved her Hello Kitty and landed on Marvin Gardens. She grimaced before dutifully forking over the appropriate amount of game cash. John instinctively counted through it.

"Dude, this is Monopoly mon—oh, wait a minute," John caught himself.

"Yeeees..." Cora said with a shifty eye. "We're playing Monopoly, John."

"Right," John smiled unsurely. "I knew that."

John rolled his dice and began to move his monster figure when The Righteous Brothers' *Unchained Melody* started up on the radio. Cora's eyes widened from behind her glasses and she jumped to her feet, simultaneously grabbing John by the arm and dragging him to his feet.

"Ow! Hey!" John protested.

"Oh, quiet down," Cora balked. "We're dancing."

Cora took John's hands and moved them into a slow dance pose. Cora's moves were smoother, but John just clunked around like he had two left feet.

"I wish you could stand on my feet so we could at least move better," Cora griped. "Or better yet, learn to dance. You move like the Tin Man."

"I'm trying to count here, Cora, so we can do this *Ghost* thing," John said, looking at his feet on the floor.

Cora looked up at John, joy completely eradicated from her face. "Please don't say that, John. It scares me."

"What?" John replied. "Relax, baby. Nothin's gonna happen to me. I'm charmed. Really," he punctuated with a comforting grin that didn't seem to work.

"Yeah, yeah, we've all seen *Tango and Cash*, John," Cora said dismissively. "And Cash got shot at the end!"

"Yeah, but it went clean through," John explained. "If you gotta get shot, that's how you want it."

"He still got shot!" Cora protested.

"Ugggh!" John groaned. "What is goin' on with you, honey?"

"Nothing," Cora tried to lie to herself. "It's... nothing." She drooped her head onto John's shoulder to try to hide her distress as Bill Medley's golden oldie singing about god sped love reached a crescendo.

CHAPTER SEVEN - Couples Therapy

The Oscob Apartment Building was one of the best middle class-oriented buildings in Klaude. While not impressive for skyscraper standards, it did stand tall amongst its concrete brethren in the city, standing a full 10 stories of apartments for those a little better off, but not entirely wealthy.

John Fetaccini and Dan Clemens stood in an elevator pulling them to their destination. Unidentifiable, generic musak played over the speakers. Clemens looked over at John, obviously impressed by the building itself.

In apartment 534, a trio of teenagers sat around a massive flat-screen television enthralled in an especially violent first-person shooter game. There was Logan, the alpha, a curly headed black-haired boy with delicate almost feminine features. Rusty, like his name indicated, was a ginger, but without the freckles. On the other side of Logan was Frog, a smaller and possibly slightly younger boy who not only sat hunched over like a frog, but also spoke in a croaking manner like one too.

John and Clemens made their way into apartment 534 where they looked especially out of place in this more extravagant setting. Clemens was closer to the kids while John took a more standoffish approach, never being too fond of children to begin with. The kids never took their eyes off the screen, barely even registering they knew they had company.

"Payment schedule," Logan asked with a dismissive laugh. "We went to public school, dude. We don't know what any a' that crap means."

"Oh right," Clemens played along. "So it's society's fault you can't pay on time."

"It's like the darkness that never leaves our hearts," Frog croaked with a laugh. The two other kids cackled in response.

"You pick that up that in English class, Frog?" Rusty asked.

"Yeah, Old Lady Rainbolt made us learn it," Frog replied.

Clemens and John looked at one another. John shook his head in confusion.

"I think we're gettin' off track, here," Clemens interjected.

"Get lost, old dudes!" Logan commanded, as if he had some authority on the situation.

"Hey guys, there's no need for insults," Clemens calmly said. "I'm just doin' my job is all."

Rusty happened to catch sight of John in the distance. "Huh? What's with that look?" he asked.

Frog turned to look as well, but Logan remained focused on the videogame. "Not that I'm gay or anything," Frog began, "but I don't think any of that goes together."

"Yeah, nice rape coat, pal," Rusty chortled.

John's reaction was negligible at best. But whether or not he didn't care or was just hiding anger very well was anyone's guess. Clemens seemed worried something was going to happen, though, and immediately turned his attention back to the kids.

"You guys've never heard of John Fetaccini?" Clemens queried.

"Who?" Rusty instinctively shot back.

"Someone famous?" Frog rhetorically asked.

"Oh yeah," Rusty said like he knew what he was talking about. "He's the big competitor with Chef Boyardee." Rusty picked up a nearby cup of water and threw it at John's hat. Clemens' mouth dropped in surprise. John silently removed his hat and wiped it clean with his free hand.

"*Aw, shit,*" Clemens thought.

"Bring us another drink, errand boy!" Logan barked.

Clemens looked back to John. He mouthed the words "errand boy" incredulously. "So these guys live in Klaude and really don't know John?" Clemens said aloud to his partner in crime. "Yep, they went to public school alright."

John took a few steps forward, once more placing his hat atop his head. "My hat was given to me by my girlfriend," he began. "It's a very nice hat and I like it very much."

Logan, his attention still fully on his video game, threw his hand dismissively to John. "Man, talk to the hand," he commanded, "cause I ain't hearin' this crap. In fact, show yourselves the fuck out of our apart—"

Logan's words were cut off by John snatching the boy's hand into his iron grasp. Clemens reacted as if it hurt him when he heard the sound of bones crunching. Immediately, Logan was yanked into the reality of the situation, as were his cohorts. He half-shouted, half-whimpered, looking at his hand.

"My hat was given to me by my girlfriend," John said bending down to speak to the purple hand as if it were a microphone. "It's a very nice hat and I like it very much."

John suddenly yanked Logan off the ground and slung him across the room. The boy crashed into the wall and upon hitting the ground, began to freak out. Frog and Rusty silently watched, their mouths scraping the floor.

"You killed my hand!" Logan whined.

"Can't say we didn't warn ya," Clemens matter-of-factly said.

Frog and Rusty scrambled for their wallets. They produced as much cash as they had on them. Clemens collected the money while John just glared at them.

"Might want to pitch in for cleaning John's hat too," Clemens suggested. Rusty forked over an extra 20 he was hiding in his pocket. Clemens took that as well.

"See, John?" Clemens smiled. "What nice, well-behaved boys we have here."

Outside, Clemens and John left the area, hoofing it down the side of a street. A smattering of cars were parked on either side of them. John rubbed one of his hands as if in pain.

"How's your hand?" Clemens asked with concern.

"Little sore," John replied. "It'll get better now that it's not bein' collided with faces."

"I don't know what Cicci was thinkin' givin' money ta kids like that," Clemens said. "No way that wasn't gonna go down any differently than it did."

"Eh, I don't have anything bad to say about Cicci," John offered. "Guy's helped me out more times than I can remember."

"Hey, I'm not sayin' nothin' bad 'bout the boss," Clemens defended. "Just think he should be more selective about who he gives money to, ya know?"

"Eh, maybe," John agreed. "Or least he could give me a percentage increase every time I have to throw somebody across a room or somethin'."

"Not unreasonable," Clemens granted.

John and Clemens moved out of the street to avoid an oncoming car. For a few moments, there was an uncomfortable silence between the two as they made their way down the street.

"Somethin' botherin' you, John?" Clemens asked. "You've been in a bit of a mood all day. Hey, if it's those mooks in the apartment, don't..."

"Naw, they're just stupid kids," John interrupted. "I dunno... You really wanna do this the rest a' your life?"

"I ain't got no appointments," Clemens shrugged. "I make alright money. Live on it. What would I do if I went out and got a real job? Cashier at McDonald's? You'd see me on the news, going all *Falling Down* on everyone and shit."

"Yeah, I bet you would," John said with a slight smile.

"Why?" Clemens asked. "You got pie-in-the-eye dreams dere, John?"

"Not really cause I can't *do* anything else," John admitted.

"Well that's pretty much why we all do this shit," Clemens explained. "None of us fit in anywhere else."

"Haven't you ever wanted to, though?" John asked.

"Fittin' in or belonging or whatever is nice," Clemens pontificated, "but it's not important. At least, I don't think so."

"Hmm..." John mumbled. "I'm goin' home, Clemens. I don't feel too well."

"Might as well," Clemens sighed. "No more work today anyway. Hell, I'd go home too if the damned neighbors weren't blarin' music all day. Don't those people work?! I mean, really."

John just looked at the ground cheerlessly as he walked on. Clemens patted him pitifully across the back.

Cora opened the door and entered her apartment, more than a little weary after a hard day's work. "Darling, I'm home!" she belted out. Cora turned around to find the apartment itself was empty and dark, far gloomier than normally. "John?" she cautiously called out.

There was no answer. Cora put her purse down on the floor and turned on the lights. The apartment was more visible now, but she felt no safer. As she looked around, Cora eventually saw a letter on the kitchen counter, held beneath the feet of an 8-inch figure of the giant monster Farmarna. Cora walked over to the letter and its monstrous guardian. The dinosaurian figure normally lived on top of the fridge, and Cora feared what the implications of its change of position had. Eventually, she pulled the letter from beneath the monster's feet. It read:

"Cora, went out. Back later."

"Goddammit, John. Don't scare me like that," Cora thought as she sighed with relief. She then looked at the monster figure as if he would provide any answers. After it remained unsurprisingly stone-lipped, Cora took the figure and set it back onto the top of the fridge where it usually stayed, guarding their food with thermonuclear fury.

Cora looked at the door as gears started to turn in her head. She then looked at her high-heeled work shoes that she'd been stomping around in since the morning. Instantaneously, she kicked them off and headed over to the closet.

John sat all alone next to an old tree at the pinnacle of a hilltop that overlooked the city's lake. Sailboats cruised in the distance. The setting sun over the cityscape horizon cast a golden hue over everything.

John looked pensive and brooding and obviously something was bothering him. He kicked listlessly at a nearby acorn. He could hear slight tromping sounds nearby but could not work up the energy to care. *"If they're some bad guy with a gun, fine, whatever,"* he thought.

But no, it was just Cora, still dressed in her lodge clothes with the exception of a pair of flat-soled sandals.

"Hey," Cora muttered.

"Hey," John muttered back. "How'd ya know I was here?"

"You weren't home," Cora explained. "I wanted to see you. Tried your favorite spot and here ya were. Bam! So simple a therapist could do it."

John forced a slight smile. Cora knelt down and sat beside him, flanking him between herself and the tree.

"Would you look at that sky?" Cora noted. "How pretty it is."

"Yeah," John agreed. "You should have seen how blue it was when the clouds weren't as visible."

"That must have been lovely," Cora surmised. "Did you walk here?"

"Yeah," John unenthusiastically replied.

"Bit of a rough walk," Cora offered.

There was a couple of seconds of silence before John turned to Cora. "How do you do it, Cora?" he asked.

"Well, we don't have a car," Cora began, "so I just had to man up and hoof it on over here. Took off my heels though. Those bitches *hurt* after a full day."

"No, not that," John shook his head. "You remember last week when we were in that Laundromat?"

"Yeah... Worst. Date. Ever," Cora said in her best Comic Book Guy voice.

"And how you were talkin' about bein' unhappy with life?" John recapped.

"Yeah?" Cora warily confirmed.

"Well, it started me thinkin'," John admitted. "I'm not very happy with the way things worked out, Cora."

Cora looked at John, overcome with surprise. "John..." she was just barely able to get it out. "Are you... are you unhappy with me?" The second between her getting that out and John's response seemed like an eternity to her, but...

"What??" John replied with equal surprise. "No, no, I love you, honey." He took Cora's hand and rubbed his thumb over its dorsum. "I'm unhappy with myself," he continued.

"Well... why? What's wrong?" Cora asked, putting a hand on his shoulder.

"Next month, I'm going to turn thirty-five," John flatly stated.

"I knew that!" Cora interjected with a shifty eye. "Who said I didn't?"

"Thirty-five," John repeated. "And look at me. I'm still doing the same ol' shit I did when I was twen'y-three."

"Twenty-three..." Cora repeated. "That's when I met you wasn't it?"

"Was it?" John replied. He wasn't even sure anymore. "I've gotta be honest with you, Cora. I never thought I'd still be around this long. I always thought I'd get gunned down in the streets Cagney-style way before now."

"John, that's a horrible thing to say!" Cora snapped back in shock. John half-heartedly shrugged. "It's just a speed bump, John," she reassured. "You'll get over it. Do you know how lucky you are?"

John turned to look at Cora. He reached up and softly touched the side of her face. "Lottery-winningly lucky," he cooed.

"That's not what I'm talkin' about," Cora replied with a smile. "But thanks. Your father left you and you came out okay. Your mother left you and you're still here. You got kicked in the throat and you still talk alright. Well, I understand you fine anyway."

"Yeah..." John wistfully answered. "You have no idea how many times I should be dead... but aren't."

"Don't say that, John," Cora said as she looked away. "It bothers me."

"I'm sorry, honey," John said as he too looked away. "It's just that... I always feel like I'm just a loser that got lucky for a while."

"That's not true," Cora said without much conviction behind it. "Don't say that."

John turned his head to look down at Cora. "Sweetie, when you were a kid, what did you wanna be when you grew up?" he asked.

"I don't know," Cora answered. "Either a rodeo clown or a zookeeper. But mostly a dancer. Or a dancing rodeo clown. That'd have been sweet."

"Why didn't you do any a' that?" John queried.

"Oh..." Cora thought. "Life just sorta happened. Besides, I'm too old to be a dancer."

"Too old? You're younger than me..." John observed.

Cora waved him off dismissively. "What did you want to be when you grew up?" she asked.

"Hugh Hefner." John quipped.

"Smooth," Cora giggled.

"I never had a real idea of anything I wanted ta do," John began. "I used ta try ta paint, but nobody liked what I did. The only thing I'm any good at is busting up people and taking money. I wanted to make a difference in someone's life. I still want that."

"What'd you paint?" Cora wondered. "I bet it was horsies."

"Anything," John answered. "I don't really remember. It was a long time ago."

"Sometimes it just takes a long time for someone to find out what they're good at, that's all," Cora said.

"You have too much faith in me, Cora," John flatly stated.

"And you have far, far too little," Cora replied. "Someone's gotta take up the slack... apparently that someone is me! But seriously, John, you're 34. There's nothing that says you have to do this your whole life. You're still at the beginning of your life. If you think of somethin' you wanna do, you can still have plenty of time to do it. Like me—I can still do anything I want, even dance maybe. But right now, I'm here to be one thing: John Fetaccini's girlfriend."

John turned to look at Cora. "I really love you," he told her.

"I love you too, John," Cora said back. "And you know you've done what you said you wanted. You've made a helluva difference in my life. In fact, you probably won't believe this, but you've made my sorry life."

"You've more than made mine," John answered. "Do you know where I'd be without you?"

"Please don't say dead, John," Cora tearfully said.

"Ever see that movie *Hobo With a Shotgun?*" John asked.

"You'd be a hobo with a shotgun?" Cora asked with confusion.

"Yeah, but without Rutger Hauer's awesomeness," John informed. "Not as glamorous anymore, is it?"

"Well, we can't all be Rutger Hauer," Cora said with a smirk.

"Ain't that the truth?" John admitted. "Hell, I'm not even Rutger from *Buffy.*"

"Since we're here and being all Lifetimey," Cora began, "can I tell you about somethin' that's been bothering me?"

"Of course, baby," John told his gal.

"Not all the time, but every so often I have these dreams," Cora explained.

"Yeah?" John inquired.

"Yeah," Cora clarified. "Actually, they're nightmares. In them, there's always something terrible has happened to you and something worse happening to me."

"Do you want to tell me about 'em?" John asked.

"No, it's okay," Cora said. "It's just scary sometimes. I use my body to make money for us and sometimes it really feels like I'm an utter whore for doing so."

"You're not a whore, Cora. You know that," John said with a twinge of anger in his voice at the suggestion.

"Yeah, I know," Cora acknowledged. "Do you remember how much of a wallflower I used ta be? Or how the girls at school said my boobs were fake? I still get catcalls when I'm out sometimes. Our culture is so drenched in sexuality that sometimes I think every guy I see on the street's going to assault me or something. It's just... I get worried with the kind of things you have to do for us that something's going to happen to you and you're going to get hurt or—"

Cora broke down and began to weep. John grabbed her and pulled her against his chest.

"Please don't cry, baby," John cooed.

"I'm not," Cora objected with a sniffle.

"It's okay, honey. It's okay," John reassured Cora as he stroked her hair.

"Is it... ?" Cora asked before snorting. "...Okay?"

"Would you like to know the sort of nightmares I have?" John offered.

"Yeah?" Cora unsurely asked.

"Well they always start with you not surviving the zombie apocalypse..." John explained.

The Zombie Apocalypse was in full swing. Chaos reigned throughout the streets of Klaude. Cars were overturned, windows knocked out, and fires intermittent. But sure enough, the grass in the city lawns were impeccably cut. The undead obviously still cared about nice-looking yards. Sounds of gunshots and shrieking permeated the air of the vicinity.

John stood in the parking lot of a ruined convenience store. He was in the middle of reloading a shotgun. Whether he was a hobo or not was indeterminable. Zombies of varying rates of deterioration shuffled about in the vicinity but they either had no interest in or didn't notice John.

However, before John slowly closing the gap between them was a zombified Cora. She growled as she stumbled forward, her arms outstretched for prey. Her clothes were sooty and ragged. Her lovely face was ruined by dead circles under her eyes, gashes and wounds of varying severity, and a rash-like bruise around her lower lip. Her eyes had turned a milky white color as if she'd gone blind.

"Cora, stop!" John commanded as he aimed his shot gun.

Zombie Cora continued to shuffle forward. "Brains!" she growled.

"You don't wanna do this, Cora," John warned. "You know what I'll do to you if you try."

"Brains!" Zombie Cora replied. Well, not so much replied, as that was all she cared about now.

John huffed, lowering his shotgun. "Last warning, Cora. I'm not kidding... I love you!"

Zombie Cora slowly dropped her arms and came to a stop. She looked straight at John as if his words had some sort of resonating meaning to her. Her lips began to quiver as if she were trying to speak on her own. But then her zombie mind took over again.

"Brains!!!" she shouted. Zombie Cora lunged at John to take a bite out of his head. But John beat her to the punch, leaping directly at her and chomping down on her neck. Zombie Cora winced with pain.

"Hey!" Zombie Cora protested in Cora's real voice. "What the hell?! Stop that!" She threw her head back to scream, but it was cut off by blood gargling out her mouth.

Back in the real world, Cora pulled away to look up at John, her eyeliner smeared by tears.

"That's not so much scary as silly," Cora declared.

"It's scary ta me," John replied. "Would it make you feel better if I taught you how to fight?"

"Would it make me feel better if you were gone but I could beat people up?" Cora sniffled. "No."

"Come on," John said defensively. "Do I look dead to you? Huh?"

"I can't even tell you how much you've done for me," Cora started. "You don't know how much better I am since you came into my life. I might have even killed myself by now."

"Oh," John said, pulling Cora into a tight embrace. "I'm sorry you had a shitty mom."

"I know," Cora responded. "You, too."

"But your dad would be so proud of the fabulous person you are," John asserted.

Cora looked up at John. Her tears could do nothing to hold back her beautiful smile. John wiped Cora's eyes clear.

"Come here," John said. He stood up and pulled Cora to her feet as well.

"Where?" Cora asked.

John and Cora walked down the hilltop and over to the shoreline of the lake. He stood beside Cora, his hands gently on her shoulders. Their images reflected on the shimmering surface of the water.

"Cora, look at the water," John instructed. "What do you see? Tell me the first thing that pops into your mind."

Cora sniffled. "Nerd. Loser. Waste a' space."

"Wow," John said with disappointment. "You really need to clean your glasses." John took Cora's glasses off her face and used his sweater to clean the lenses. He then put them back onto her face. She adjusted them to fit correctly.

"Look carefully," John said. "Whaddaya see?"

"I don't know," Cora replied. "What am I supposed to see? What do you see?"

"It doesn't matter what I see," John stated. "What do *you* see?"

Cora looked at the reflection. After a moment or two passed, she cocked her head as if something struck her.

"You want to know what I see?" Cora asked.

"Yes." John said enthusiastically. "Tell me."

"I see a strong, devoted couple that beat the odds and showed my fucking shrew of a mother what's what," Cora declared. "I see a couple who may not have found their place in the world but have found their place with each other. And most importantly, I see a couple of people who might not be much on their own, but together, form a whole unit."

"Wow," John said, completely taken aback. "That's a lot better than what'd I'd come up with."

Cora laughed. And smiled.

"I like you better when you're laughing," John said.

"Me too, John," Cora agreed. "Me too."

John and Cora slowly turned and began up the hill. John reached out and put his hand around Cora's back and Cora responded by doing the same.

"This is the end..." John began to sing. Or at least talk in a sort-of sing-y fashion. "Hold your breath and count to ten. Feel the earth move and then. Hear my heart burst again."

Cora knew she had to join in. And did.

"Let the sky fall. When it crumbles... we will stand tall... Face it all together. Let the sky fall. When it crumbles... we will stand tall... Face it all together... At Skyfall... At Skyfall..."

They sounded so much better together than John had when he was singing by himself.

John and Cora were still singing as he carried her newlywed-style up the stairs to their apartment. But by now, it was the main theme from *Moonraker* being belted out as a duet.

The door lock rattled and the door swung open to reveal John carrying Cora through the doorway. He turned on the nearby light switch with his elbow, illuminating the apartment, before setting Cora onto her feet. They laughed to themselves as John closed and locked the door behind him.

"It sure got dark fast, didn't it?" Cora observed.

"I'm surprised it stayed light as long as it did," John replied.

Cora went into the kitchen to get a drink of water. John stood there and watched her as she moved. He then noticed the top of the fridge.

"I see you put Farmarna back," John commented.

"What?" Cora looked up, then over at the fridge. "Oh yeah. You never know what food bandits might raid the place while we're gone."

John laughed to himself. "Are you okay, Cora?" he asked.

"What?" Cora responded, drinking from the faucet.

"Are you okay?" John repeated. "Really okay?"

"Yeah. I think so," Cora answered, turning off the sink.

John nodded. He then turned and started towards the bedroom.

"John?" Cora quietly said. He stopped and turned back to face her.

"I don't even know how to hit," Cora admitted.

"Do you wanna know?" John queried.

"Yeah, alright," Cora said, still unsure of herself.

CHAPTER EIGHT -
Rage and Fury Signifying Nothing

It was an overcast, windy day over the Puptown Gentlemen's Club's rooftop. Even the clouds seemed to be shying away from the cold. John was there in all his street finery as was Cora, dressed in a light red hoodie and a thin powder-blue T-shirt reading *Anything Not Related to Elephants is Irrelephant*. She was visibly cold. Also present were Dan Clemens and the scroungy-looking fellow known as Hornsby.

"I didn't know it'd be this cold up here," Cora shivered. "I'd have worn something warmer."

"Clemens, would you go down and see if we got anything warmer for Cora to put on?" John asked.

"Sure thing, John," Clemens said with a wave.

Clemens headed for the rooftop exit at the edge of the roof. John turned to Hornsby. "Now, Hornsby, are you *sure* you want to do this?" he asked.

"Fuck yeah!" Hornsby replied. "Cicci says I don't owe him anymore for doin' this. I am in."

"Alright, man," John said. "Just so you know, we're not doing this to be mean and we're not forcing you to do this. You made this choice, okay?"

"I'm a big boy, Fetaccini," Hornsby retorted.

"Alright," John unsurely said. He then turned back to Cora.

"John, you didn't tell me I'd have to actually hit somebody," Cora said, gesturing to Hornsby.

"It's the best way to learn," John informed. "Punching bags and stuff like that are alright, but there's nothing like actually hitting another person. Think about it, when was the last time a punching bag started shit with you?"

Cora stood there, actually thinking about some past event. "Well, there was that one time..." she pondered aloud.

"But if you hit an actual person," John continued, "you're going to be ready for it and know what to expect, when you really have to hit somebody... which I hope you never do."

"Well..." Cora surmised. "Could come in handy next time you're handing my ass to me in *Mario Kart*."

"Now, that is not cool," John protested.

"Yeah, yeah," Cora dismissed him.

"Um, are we gonna do this?" Hornsby curtly asked. Cora turned and looked back at John.

"So go up to him and punch him," John instructed.

Cora marched straight up to Hornsby and gave him a closed-fisted tap on the chest. John rolled his eyes in disappointment. Hornsby looked down at his chest, then to Cora, and lastly over to John. "Ow?" he said with a shrug.

"Well, come on," Cora defended. "I'm not mad at him. How am I supposed really hit him if I'm not angry?"

"Yeah and you're not punching right," John stated.

"'I'm not punching right'? There's a wrong way to punch?" Cora said dubiously.

"Yeah," John answered. "Hit him again. But this time put some force behind it," he said with an illustrative punch at the air.

"Okay..." Cora said, unsure of herself.

Cora punched Hornsby again, this time with only rudimentary more force. The only real reaction given was by Cora, withdrawing and shaking her hand in pain.

"Ow!" Cora whined. "How do you do this?"

John marched over to Cora and Hornsby's position. He took hold of her hand.

"You're doing what a lot of people do," John continued with the lesson. "You have to hit with your knuckles, not your fingers."

"Not my fingers?" Cora clarified.

"Yeah. See, make a fist," John directed.

Cora held up her hand in a clinched fist.

"Okay, look. You're connecting with the fingers part of your hand," John said, running his fingers across Cora's hand. "All that does is hurt you because fingers aren't meant to be smashed on impact. See your knuckles here? Those are what you want to make contact with the other person. *Those* are what will clean somebody's clock. Now, try it again."

Cora took a breath, then drew back and punched Hornsby once again.

"Egh..." Hornsby reacted.

"Good!" John reinforced. "See how that didn't really hurt?"

"Yeah!" Cora realized.

"But you need more force behind the punch," John observed, again throwing a punch to illustrate the point.

"John? If I may?" Hornsby interrupted. The scraggly man looked Cora over, perhaps a little too luridly, then let out a wolf-whistle. "You look pretty good on them getaway sticks, baby! Maybe they'd look better wrapped around my head."

Cora's good humor immediately leapt out the window.

"How'd you like to hop on my elephant?" Hornsby leched, ogling the top part of Cora's t-shirt.

"Hey! Ease up there," John chided.

Hornsby probably should have listened. But instead, he proceeded to proclaim, "Your tits. My mouth. Let's make this happen."

Cora suddenly hauled off and punched Hornsby flush on the chin, sending him collapsing to the ground. But before he was even flat on the rooftop, Cora was on him with a furious assault of punches, some thrown sloppier than the others.

"My fist. Your dick. Let's make *that* happen!" Cora barked, raining down punches on Hornsby.

"Cora! Cora! Chill out!" John shouted, attempting to calm her down.

Clemens returned from the rooftop exit with a man's white dress shirt. "No sweaters or nothin' down there, but we did have this dress shirt..." he stopped short as he saw Cora sitting on the sprawled Hornsby beating the living hell out of him.

"Cora! Calm down!" John shouted. "He didn't mean it!" John grabbed hold of Cora from behind, trying to pull her away.

Clemens rushed over as fast as he could to help. He and John finally succeeded in yanking Cora off the unconscious bastard.

"John, what the hell did he do to her?!" Clemens demanded to know.

Cora slowly regained her composure, but continued to breathe heavily.

"I'm... I'm sorry, Dan," Cora said, wiping the hair out of her eyes.

"Eh, Hornsby got a little mouthy," John explained.

Clemens looked down on the ground at the bloodied Hornsby. "I don't think that's gonna be a problem anymore. Hell, we may owe *him* a few dollars..." he observed.

"I'm so sorry, John," Cora said turning back to face him.

"It's okay," John said reassuringly. "That's what happens when you hit somebody. Or whale on 'em as the case may be."

"He's not dead, is he?" Cora wondered.

"Clemens?" John asked.

Clemens looked back to John. "I look like a doctor over here?" he snapped.

"Well, you could check his pulse," John suggested.

Clemens bent down and felt Hornsby's throat for a few seconds. He looked back to John and Cora. "Yeah, he'll live."

"I'm gonna get Cora outta here," John said. "Can you take care a' him for us?"

"No sweat, John," Clemens replied. "I'm kinda scared about what she'll do to me if I don't."

Cora smirked as John turned her around and they began heading for the rooftop's exit.

"I don't ever want to do that again," Cora said, ashamed of herself.

"Hmm... Do you feel any better knowing you can do that if you need to?" John inquired.

"Yeah, I kinda do," Cora realized. She then stopped and faced John with a dour expression on her face and a clinched fist at her side. "Are you gonna take the trash out tonight?"

"Aw, hell!" John groaned. "Is this how's it gonna be now?"

Cora laughed and lightly tapped John in the shoulder. "Oh! Wait, John!" she excitedly said. "Take a picture with me to commemorate my first beatdown."

"Be-uh... okay," John unsurely responded.

Cora pulled out her cell phone from her purse and held it out to take a selfie.

"Hold on," John interrupted. "Hold up your other hand, it'll make you look dangerous," he said, holding up his own fist to demonstrate. Cora followed suit and happily clicked off a photo.

The next Friday, a crowd of moviegoers stood in line at the theater waiting to buy tickets. On the marquee—in addition to *The UPS vs. the Federal Express*—

were other new openings such as *Kittens and Nazis*, *More Trouble in Little China*, *The Ten Commandments of Dracula*, *Old Habits Die Hard*, and *How the Grinch Stole Angela's Ashes* as well as a re-release of the late 90s hit *When Dirty Harry Met Sally*.

John and Cora sat in the upper echelons of the theater showing the Stallone/Schwarzenegger UPS/Fed-Ex grudge match. Cora's head was reclined on John's shoulder as she merrily munched popcorn situated in John's lap.

The crowd in the movie, what could be made out of them, were mostly of an older generation, 40-50 year olds. John and Cora seemed to be some of the youngest viewers on hand. The theater was permeated by the sounds of movie gunshots, explosions, crowd cheers or laughs, along with onscreen muttering of Austrian and New York accents.

Frankie, Beanie, and Sam entered the theater from the bottom, loudly talking to each other about some incident outside. They were dressed to the nines in gangsta fashion. Light from the movie screen even flashed off their considerable bling.

"Will you watch where the hell you goin'?!" Beanie intimidated as they searched for seats.

Several audience members were already bothered by the trio's disturbance. Eventually, the three hooligans found their way to three empty seats down the row from John and Cora. They immediately plopped their tennis-shoed feet on the chairs in front of them, much to the chagrin of the people in the row below them. Sam yanked out his cell phone and began to check his messages, lighting up the immediate area around them. John and Cora looked down at them; Cora was especially unnerved.

"Phil, get to de choppa!" a voice from the movie shouted out, followed by an especially loud explosion that lit up the crowd.

"Aw, hell yeeeeeeeeeeeah!" Frankie loudly cheered.

"That's what I came ta see!" Beanie joined in.

"Shhh!" hissed some member of the audience.

Sam looked over to his compatriots with his cell phone to his ear. "Hey, you guys better quiet down," he obliviously said.

"Oh, I don't give a fuck!" Frankie proclaimed. "These bitches don't know how to have a good time."

Cora rolled her head from John's shoulder to her side in disgust. John took note, then looked down at the three kids.

"Hey, why don't you guys shut up down there?" John demanded more than asked, grabbing their especially unwanted attention.

"What?" Beanie smugly said, deliberately baiting John.

"What'?" John repeated their question, as he rose to his feet. "Maybe you'll hear me a little better with my foot in yer ass... since it's obvious that's where yer head is."

"Man, sit yo' bitch ass down," Frankie threatened, "before we—"

"What?" John interrupted. "Mouth off at me again? Why don't you punks get ta steppin', and let us watch the damned movie? You know, we who actually paid to see it instead a' wanderin' in from another one?"

Sam shifty eyed from John to the other two as if he were in the middle of a spaghetti western standoff.

Beanie shot to his feet. "Man, you don't tal—"

Suddenly a flashlight beam rested on Beanie's face. An usher was making his way up the stairs into the back. His features couldn't be made out in the darkness, but he certainly spoke authoritatively enough.

"Excuse me, you three," the usher began. "You'll have to come with me. You're causing too much of a disturbance."

"Man, fuck all y'all!" Beanie shouted, flopping his arms about. "C'mon!"

Beanie, Frankie, and Sam got up and began to exit the theater, followed by the usher. John sat back down.

"Man, enjoy your faggoty-ass movie, dumb bitches!" Frankie shouted.

"You punks better have tickets for this," the usher said.

The three kids and the usher disappeared around a corner, causing a sparse section of the audience to applaud. Cora snuggled back up to John.

"You didn't need to do that, ya know," Cora quietly said.

"If I didn't who would?" John whispered. Cora slightly shrugged then resumed eating popcorn.

"Ah'll be bahk..." a voice from the movie said, followed by a massive explosion. John chuckled, but Cora merely rolled her eyes.

"Really, Arnold?" Cora quietly muttered as she shook her head.

The doors of the theater opened up and patrons spilled out from within. Amongst them were John and Cora, arm in arm. They appeared to be fairly mollified by what they had seen.

"So, you know what we need to do?" Cora asked.

"What's that?" John replied.

"Steal a time machine..." Cora began. "Go back to 1988... and get Sly and Arnold to star in... *Contra: The Movie.*" She gestured the title as she spoke it.

"Oh, hell yes!" John agreed. "You know where we can find one?"

"Mmm. I was hoping you did," Cora disappointedly answered.

Outside, Beanie, Frankie, and Sam were loitering about despite the presence of at least two *No Loitering* signs posted. Sam nudged Frankie and pointed to the theater doors, revealing John and Cora exiting the complex. The trio mobilized and headed for them.

"Well it was better than that last Merchant-Ivory film you dragged me to," John declared. "And I do believe you still owe me some head for that one."

"Yeah, yeah," Cora waved him off. "Later tonight... perhaps."

"Hey, enjoy the movie, bitch-ass punk?" Beanie shouted as he and his friends closed in the gap betwixt the five. John and Cora looked up to see who was speaking, but then ignored them and continued on their way.

"Hey, why you leavin' with him, bitch?" Frankie aggressively asked Cora. "You know you'd be a lot happier straddlin' BBC pipe!" The boy bit his lip and made thrusting gestures with his pelvis.

Cora looked back at the three, smiling and waving. "Eat shit and die!" she cheerily told them.

"Whoo, listen to the mouth on that bitch!" Beanie retorted.

"Need to bitchtame that ho!" Frankie observed, making a whip noise to punctuate it. "Black dat ass inta next week!"

John stopped completely in his tracks. Cora was jerked backwards by his sudden halt. She tried to pull him along with her, but he refused to budge.

"Come on, John," she pleaded. "It's okay. Let's just go."

John turned towards the three kids, leaving Cora behind.

"Come on, John. Don't..." Cora implored but it fell on deaf ears. John walked straight over to the three boys.

"Whatchu want, bitch?" Frankie challenged, apparently unable to properly size up the situation.

John slammed a right hook into Frankie's face, followed by a couple of gut shots, and a cross to the chin that sent the punk sprawling to the ground.

"First, asshole," John growled.

Beanie's fist slammed into the side of John's head, doing nothing more than infuriating him. Before he knew it, John's boot was buried in Beanie's stomach. Suddenly, Cora slammed her purse against the back of Beanie's head. The kid dropped to the pavement like a sack of potatoes, a whimpering mess. John turned to the watching Sam, who was still apparently messing with his cell phone.

"Anybody else wanna play winner?" John asked as he put his arm around a triumphant-looking Cora.

Sam slowly shook his head, in wide-eyed surprise. Cora turned to John and took his head in her hands. "Oh, John, are you okay?" she asked.

"Yeah, I'm fine," John reassured. "Just some kids, you know, playin' around. C'mon."

Cora gave one last look back to the three kids as she and John left them behind. Frankie was groaning in pain, while Beanie was completely knocked out.

"You play too rough, John," Cora noted.

While Sam had gone home, Beanie and Frankie managed to drag their busted-up selves back to Proton and Crimilicious' neighborhood. A couple of kids were sitting on the hood of a parked BMW with the hull raised off the ground and the tires coated in shiny, chrome rims. A baseline pumped from an indeterminable origin nearby.

Crimilicious sat in the backseat of the parked BMW, writing something down on a sheet of paper, using a street light to see. Across from him sat Beanie and in the front seat was Frankie, skulking with a large bandage gauze plastered around his forehead.

"...an' this punk iced Frankie an' broke two a' my ribs," Beanie tattled.

"Who was it?" Crimilicious queried without looking up.

"I dunno," Frankie admitted. "Some eye-talian. Had some real good-lookin' bitch with him."

"Well, what in the hell were you doin' makin' all that noise in a theater?" Crimilicious admonished. "Damn, man! Ya know it ain't yer livin' room. People're tryin' ta watch a movie."

"It was Sam makin' most a' the noise," Beanie lied.

"I don't care whose fault it was!" the boss man snapped. "But I can't be havin' people think we're just a bunch of punks down here. Get some cats together and go drive-by those foos in Puptown."

"On it," Frankie shot back like he couldn't wait.

"Yo, what you so busy with over there, Crimilicious?" Beanie questioned, bending over to better see.

"I'm tryin' ta figure out my grocery list here," Crimilicious revealed.

CHAPTER NINE - Hello and Goodbye

The following Monday, several cars drove by the outside of the inconspicuous-looking Puptown Gentlemen's Club as the sun shone down, bathing the surrounding area in a warming golden hue. Most of Cicci's crew were present inside, playing pool or cards, or just talking amongst themselves, waiting for their boss to assign them a job for the day.

John Fetaccini sat at a table figuring something with pencil and paper. He sipped from a coffee mug that said *WTF* across it as he worked on finances to do something for Cora. As such, it was so important that John couldn't take any chances with numerical mistakes, so he broke out his eyeglasses to better see numbers with.

Cicci walked over to the table, bringing with him one Robert Seger, a young man around 27 years old who was dressed up in his finest Sunday church clothes.

"Hey, John," Cicci spoke up to get his attention.

John craned his neck slightly and looked up to see who was coming towards him. He took his glasses off and hid them in the recesses of his coat as Cicci and Robert sat down nearby.

"I'd like you to meet a new recruit," Cicci began. "This here's Robert Seger."

"How ya doin'?" John questioned with a warm smile and nod.

"Pretty good," Robert replied. "Yourself?"

"Can't complain," John answered. "Every day above ground is a good day." Cicci grinned slightly.

Something hit John out of the blue and he suddenly turned to Robert with a perplexed expression.

"Wait a minute..." John said like someone cheated him out of some money. "Your name's Bob Seger??"

"*Robert*," the younger man curtly answered. "My parents are idiots."

"That's not nice," Cicci interjected.

"Yeah," John agreed. "*Night Moves* is great for the end of a date."

Robert made no further reaction.

"I want you to take Robert here aroun' with you to show 'im how we do things aroun' here," Cicci spoke up. "Break him in slowly, ya know?"

"Sure, whatever you say," John nodded. "We'll go get some money in a minute. Cicci's always got somebody that owes him somethin' and we collect, got it?"

"Got it," Robert repeated.

"Good," John replied. "Now just lemme finish this an' we'll be on our way."

As John went back to his figuring, Cicci rose to his feet.

"John, I gotta get goin'," the boss man explained. "I got an appointment elsewhere so I will be seein' ya. Talk to ya later, eh?"

"Sure, Cicci!" John looked up to acknowledge his boss' leaving. "See ya!"

As Cicci turned and headed for the exit, a very slick-looking shiny black Civic tricked out with raised shocks passed by the street outside. Automatic-fire gunshots rang out from the open windows. The bullets broke several of the club's windows as people inside hit the dirt. Cicci, however, wasn't so lucky and was riddled with gunfire, which sent crimson sprays into the surrounding air. After his body hit the ground, Cicci's blood stained the floor as it ran from his bullet holes.

Robert leapt across the table he was sitting at and pushed John onto the floor as a spray of bullets hit the table top where they were sitting. Sarrageno and Clemens ran for the broken windows, absentmindedly passing over Cicci's corpse as they wildly aimed their pistols and shot return fire as the Civic sped away outside.

John was flattened across the ground with Robert laying on top of him. The two slowly raised their heads and looked around the immediate area.

"You okay?" Robert asked.

"Get off me!" John hissed as he waved the younger man off.

John and Robert as well as others in the room rose to their feet in a slightly en masse manner. Turning away from the window, Clemens noticed who was lying on the ground. "Oh, Jesus Christ..." the rattled gangster mumbled.

John looked over and saw Cicci lying on the floor. Everyone in the immediate area ran over to his corpse.

"Somebody call an ambulance!" Sarrageno belted out to no one in particular.

John's eyes widened and his face dropped with silent rage as he noticed Cicci wasn't breathing. He turned and began to kick any chairs unlucky enough to be nearby across the room and even turned and punched a hole in the wall.

"John..." an onlooker futilely tried to get his attention. "John, calm down!"

Suddenly, John whirled around and grabbed Robert by the shoulder. "You wanna see what we do?" he stated more than asked, scaring Robert with his intensity. "Here's your chance."

John pulled Robert with him as he stormed out of the Gentlemen's Club, leaving everyone else behind to deal with the mess. None of them really knew what to do from there. It was if their collective head had been cut off.

Later that night, Cicci's crew met in an old warehouse downtown. They did favors for the night watchman sometimes, so he let them in without a word. The gangsters were huddled around in a circle, amongst crowds of nondescript crated cargo. While Vinelli, Sarrageno, Clemens, and Robert were on hand, so were several other of Cicci's men including Remo, a short, squat fellow, Gagi, a thin rail of a man with a gaunt face, De Luna, a bespectacled man in an overcoat, and Sabelli, an overweight man with a wrinkly pushed-in face.

"So what are we gonna do about Cicci, guys?" Vinelli broke the ice.

"Well, what can we do?" Gagi questioned. "He's dead, God rest his soul."

"Damned shame," Sabelli offered.

"We gotta bigger problem than that," Clemens began to point out. "Who's gonna be boss now?"

"Clemens, you're pretty smart," De Luna shouted out. The surrounding men murmured in agreement. Clemens shook his head and waved his hands. He was having none of it.

"You should think about John Fetaccini," Robert spoke up. The others immediately shut up and looked at him as if to ask "who are you, new guy?"

"Well, I-I mean..." Robert stammered, "you should have seen him this morning. He was kickin' everybody's ass, trying to find out something about all this. And when he went to collect, he pulled his gun four times. I don't think any of 'em were even packing!"

"Guess today wasn't a day to fuck around with John," Gagi postulated.

"That it wasn't," Robert concurred.

"John's not full Italian," Sabelli pointed out.

"So?" Robert inquired.

"I think Cicci would've wanted him," Vinelli thought aloud.

"Yeah, I think so, too," Gagi admitted. "The old-school rules aren't really relevant any more."

Sarrageno turned to Clemens, who was visibly lost in thought. "Clemens, what do you think?" he point-blank asked.

Clemens took a deep breath. "It seems to me," he began, "that John would be a damned good boss. I mean, whenever Cicci did something, John was there."

"Hey, where is John anyway?" De Luna inquired as if he'd just now noticed he was missing.

"I dunno," Sarrageno answered. "I haven't seen 'im since he left this mornin'."

"He told me he was goin' home and to report back anything that went down," Robert explained.

"And where's Dimi?" Remo shrugged, looking around. "I ain't seen him all day at all."

"Ah, he'll turn up," Clemens waved him off. "So... are we in agreement that John's the new boss?"

Everyone let out a simultaneous "aye."

"The ayes have it," Clemens continued.

"Anybody know when the funeral is?" Vinelli questioned.

"Funeral home said Friday at 2:00," Sabelli replied.

"I guess we'll have to make a trip to the floral shop, huh?" De Luna observed.

The gang began to laugh as they split up, the meeting apparently over.

"Those damned florists are crooks," Clemens complained as he sauntered away.

Around this same time back in his apartment, a forlorn and defeated John Fetaccini lie on the couch with his head in Cora's lap. She was wearing a black house dress with an unbuttoned, red, wool sweater over her shoulders and no shoes. Cora softly rubbed the side of John's head as he looked dead-eyed into the distance.

"Oh, it's all over," John sighed. "Everything. All gone."

"What's gone, hon?" Cora asked.

"Without a boss, everybody'll be just wanderin' around like a buncha zombies," the collector explained. "Everything'll fall apart and we'll probably all end up bein' pinched. Berlin was right: it *is* just a matter of time."

"Don't you think that's jumping to extremes, John?" Cora queried, leaning over in hopes she could see John's face better. She could not. He was so out of it that he didn't even notice that her boobs were resting on the side of his head. Cora leaned into her sitting posture again, taken aback by his lack of reaction to her attempt to bait him out of his funk. "*This is really serious*," she thought. "Wasn't there someone behind Cicci?" she pressed.

"He wasn't expecting this, so he never named a successor," John flatly replied.

Cora bit her lip at a loss for words.

"The breakdown's already begun, Cora," John began. "People everywhere heard about Cicci and already think they ain't gotta pay up. And this is just the tip of the iceberg."

Cora bent down and kissed John on the side of his head. He blinked his eyes, then rolled around to face her.

"It's gonna be okay, John," Cora reassured.

"Is it?" John wondered aloud. "I'm unconvinced. I... I don't want this."

"Nobody does," Cora said softly. "But I'm glad you're here. And I'm thankful you're safe and that it wasn't you. I'll take sad John over dead John any day."

John sat up, but whirled around and sort of straddled Cora. "I love you, Cora Secillia" he muttered, resting his forehead on hers.

"I love you, John Fetaccini," Cora shot back.

The two began to slowly kiss. Tongues found their way around the other in no time. Several loud knocks on the door interrupted them. John and Cora pulled away, each with disappointment etched across their faces.

"You think if we ignore 'em, they'll go away?" John questioned.

More knocks at the door followed.

"Probably not," Cora admitted.

With a sigh, John climbed off Cora and the couch and got to his feet. Cora took note of something and her eyes widened in realization.

"John," Cora called out. "My lipstick's on your mouth!"

"Huh??" John grunted.

He quickly wiped his mouth with the palm of his hand until there was no more lipstick there. He then moved over to the door, unlocked it and opened it. Standing just outside were Sarrageno and Clemens.

"John!" Sarrageno greeted warmly. "We're glad you're here."

"Why?" John glibly replied.

Clemens cleared his throat. "Could you come out here for a moment?" he asked.

John looked back at Cora before stepping out of his apartment and closing the door behind him. Once outside, he noted Sabelli and Gagi at the bottom of the stairs keeping a lookout. For what he wasn't sure.

Clemens turned and looked to see no one was around and then turned back to John. "Well, we all got together and decided that you should be the new boss," he announced.

"Oh, come on, guys," John shot back. "You can do better'n me. Geno's pretty smart, ya know," he gestured to his associate. Sarrageno gave an "aw shucks" response.

"No, John," Clemens began. "We decided you'd be the best man."

"Why me?" John inquired.

"Cause it's what Cicci would've wanted," Sarrageno replied. Clemens nodded. John looked at the two gangsters. He looked at the men downstairs. He wondered if it was possible to stop being so... illegitimate.

"Okay," John almost barely got out. Clemens and Sarrageno were visibly relived.

"Good," Sarrageno said.

"You gonna be in tomorrow?" Clemens queried.

"No," John stated. "Wait, yeah."

"We'll see ya tomorrow, then... Boss," Clemens replied.

"See ya, Clemens, Geno," John waved. "Sabelli, Gagi," he pointed at the men downstairs. They waved back before opening up the door to outside and disappeared behind it. John opened the door to his apartment and followed suit. Cora was still sitting on the couch as if she were waiting for bad news.

"Well," John began as he locked the door once again. "Something happened."

"What?" Cora asked, now particularly doe-eyed.

John moved his mouth to the side in thought. "I'm the boss now," he answered.

"I toldja it was gonna be okay," Cora informed.

"I know," John agreed. "I shoulda listened to you, Cora. You're so smart."

"Sometimes," Cora grinned.

CHAPTER TEN -
First Day on the Job All Over Again

The following morning, sunlight crept in through the curtains of John and Cora's bedroom. The two lay in bed facing one another. The covers on John's side of the bed were a strewn-about mess while they were generally more kempt on Cora's side.

The sun entering the room managed to wake John from his slumber. His eyes flickered slowly to see Cora just ahead of him. He could hear her breathing and it sounded like the most soothing of music to him. "*Today may not be so bad*," he thought to himself.

Suddenly, the alarm clock on a nearby table went off indicating that it was 6:00. Cora began to slowly stir, but before she was fully awake, John had reached over and hit the top of the clock to cease its intrusion.

Cora's eyes slowly opened and she saw John receding back from shutting off the alarm.

"Thank you, John," the half-awake woman muttered. "I hate you, 6 a.m."

"It is a cruel bastard," John added.

"It is indeed," Cora sighed. She started to climb out of bed to begin her morning ritual, but John reached out to gently clamp his hands around her to keep her in bed. Cora smiled at the futility of his gesture.

"I have to get ready for work," Cora balked, her eyes still closed.

"No, I'm not letting you go," John replied. "It's too early ta get outta bed."

"That's the truth," Cora agreed before letting out a yawn.

"You're so cute when you're half-asleep like this," John observed.

Cora's eyes suddenly opened. She turned her head to look over at John. "Why are you being extra cute this morning?"

John didn't really want to tell her that he didn't want her to go to work. And he didn't want to tell her that he didn't either. Instead, he opted to clamp his mouth around hers for a kiss. As he pulled away, Cora grimaced as she tasted her own morning breath.

"That couldn't have been particularly nice," Cora observed, her eyes closed again. "Neither of us have brushed our teeth."

"I don't care," John shot back.

Cora smiled again. Her arms finally began to push her toward the edge of the bed to get up. John grabbed her and pulled her back into the middle of the bed, wrapping his arms around her as best he could. Under the covers, he wrapped a leg around hers.

"You can't get up," John declared. "You're my prisoner today."

Cora half-grinned again and silently laughed. "That sounds wonderful... but I hafta go to work."

"You don't have to," John argued.

"Money, bills, food," Cora mumbled, half-asleep again.

"I could have the boys go over an' have a talk with yer boss," John suggested.

"Probably not the best of ideas," Cora admitted. "I'll tell you what—ten more minutes, then I *have* to go. That's the best deal I can give you."

"Fine," the collector grumbled.

"Love you," Cora said in her cutest voice.

"Love you more," John answered, before resting his forehead onto hers.

Later that morning, closer to 10:00, John, in his street walkin' finery, entered the doors of the Puptown Gentlemen's Club to find Sarrageno, Clemens, Vinelli, Robert, Remo, Sabelli, and De Luna already there. As they took note of his sudden appearance, they all let out warm greetings to their new boss.

"I don't suppose we have somebody on these windows here," John spoke up, acknowledging the bullet holes still in the club's windows.

"Got somebody comin' by this afternoon," De Luna answered.

"This guy is on top a' things," John said, snapping his fingers and pointing at De Luna for punctuation. "What else we got?"

"Not much, John," Remo admitted.

"Well, shit," the new boss hissed.

"I heard somethin' 'bout a guy stayin' over at the Crescent Moon Hotel that might have been in on it," Sabelli spoke up.

"Crescent Moon?" John queried. "Who?"

"We're not sure who this guy is," Sabelli responded. "But we got eyes on 'im."

"Good job," the new boss said. "You know what room he's in?"

"Might've been One-Twenny-Four," Sabelli half-wondered aloud. "Or maybe it was 214... yeah, definitely 214."

"You sure?" John asked for clarification.

"Yeah, I'm sure," Sabelli said more confidently. "214."

"Okay," John began, looking around the Gentlemen's Club. "Geno and Clemens, you come with me. The rest a' you guys just make the usual rounds, and try an' get any dirt ya can. Okay? Let's go."

John clapped his hands together like a football coach, then turned and walked off with Sarrageno and Clemens in tow. The rest milled about watching the three march off.

In Crimilicious' living room, he, Ty, and Jerome were all kicked back on the various gaudy-looking sofas and couches he had scattered about the room. They were watching *New Jack City* at an unreasonable volume on television. However, Jerome's attention had been pulled away from the movie as he looked over a large, crystal paperweight.

"I just don't get this at all," Jerome thought aloud.

Crimilicious looked over to his compatriot's direction. "Yo, man, it holds down sheets a' paper so they don't blow away in a breeze," he explained. "Don't take no rocket scientist to figa that one out."

"Whaa... ? No, dawg!" Jerome retorted, putting the paperweight down. "Your boys fuckin' kill Colone and Fetaccini does nothin' but sit on his ass. What's that all about?"

"Fetaccini?" Ty scoffed. "Piss on 'im, huh?"

"Unless you see him in Proton," Crimilicious dismissed his pal's concerns, "I say don't sweat it."

"Hey, you say piss on him—" Jerome began.

"I did *not* say that," Crimilicious interrupted, holding up a finger.

"But I'm tellin' ya this Fetaccini's a rough guy," Jerome continued. "You hear about him bitchin' up Marty the other day?"

"Will you guys shut up?" Crimilicious demanded more than asked. "I can't hear the damned movie here. Besides, it don't take Sam Jackson to bitch up Marty. Fetaccini may be a rough mook, but you guys know all it takes is a coupla bats to turn today's bad muthafucka into yesterday's bitch."

"Man, I miss beatin' on chumps with bats," Ty wistfully commented. "Don't get to do that so much anymore since everyone started packin'."

Crimilicious turned to Ty with an incredulous "you're kidding" look on his face.

"I'm tellin' ya," Jerome still fretted. "Shit's gonna rain down if you don't do somethin'."

"Big deal," Crimilicious sneered. "If Colone would have been tighter with his security, he'd still be alive today. Fetaccini's no different," he stated looking over at Jerome.

"Look, if he worries you that much, get rid a' 'im. Now can we get back to the movie please?"

Crimilicious' partners in crime finally clammed up in time for them to see Wesley Snipes nonchalantly sitting on a throne watching *Scarface* on his own television within the movie.

Cars passed by outside the Crescent Moon Hotel, a rather unassuming spot that looked like it was built with motel sensibilities in a hotel's structure. Only a few vehicles were sprinkled about the parking lot.

Room 214 was unusually filled with visitors today. John, Sarrageno, and Clemens had managed to make their way there. Sarrageno stood guard at the door. A younger man named Juan Ortega was tied to a chair in the middle of the room. He was a Hispanic fellow in his mid-twenties with dark, black hair. He was incredibly scared as John paced up and down the room with a baseball bat resting over his shoulder. The room itself, however, was an utter mess, betraying the fight that had apparently broken out there.

"Mr. Fetaccini," Ortega haltingly began. "I told deez guys I don't know nuthin' and they don't believe me—"

Clemens reached over and slapped Ortega on the back of the head. "Shut that hole, mook," he ordered.

John turned back to face the frightened boy. "Do you know who I am?" he questioned.

"Yeah, you're John Fetaccini," Ortega answered. "You're the new boss over in Puptown now."

"Man, news travels fast, eh, Clemens?" John observed. "That's right. And do you know what I'm gonna do ta ya if you're lyin' ta me?"

"You're gonna knock a homerun on my head with that bat," Ortega surmised.

"That's right, I am," John confirmed. "So try speaking in words instead of your damned, dirty lies. Now, tell me who ordered the hit on Cicci."

"I don't know," Ortega replied impotently.

"Who was it?!" John demanded to know, swinging back to severely hurt Ortega with the bat.

"I don't know!" Ortega half-shouted, half-whined.

"Who did it, you rat motherfucker?!" the new boss shouted. "Who set Cicci up?!" He was a heartbeat away from knocking Ortega's head out the window.

"Alright! Alright" the frightened boy said to stop them. It succeeded and John paused, slightly lowering the bat. "It was Crimilicious!" Ortega finally snitched. "Crimilicious did it! That guy Dimi's workin' for Crimilicious on the side and they did the hit on Cicci! Something about 'teachin' you wops a lesson'. I don't know. One a' your guys beat up some of theirs. That's all I know! I swear to you on my mother's life!"

John thought it over. He wasn't exactly sure whether he should hit the kid or believe him.

"What do you want us to do, John?" Clemens inquired after a few moments.

John stood there silently for a moment. "Let 'im go," he finally spoke up. "He told us all we need ta know."

John threw the bat to the floor with palpable disdain, then turned and marched out of the room. Sarrageno opened the room's door for him to pass through and closed it behind him.

Ortega, meanwhile, was relieved at John's decision. "That was fuckin' trippy," he said to the others remaining in the room.

Clemens slapped the younger man in the back of the head again. "You got lucky, cocksucker," he warned. "Don't push it."

John charged down the hallway, incensed at the information he'd just been given. He knew Dimi was an asshole, but never imagined he was this much of an asshole. He'd have to be made an example of if they could find him. John came to the stairwell entrance and opened the door.

Just as he entered into the stairwell, John heard the noise of people approaching from below. He inched his head over the side of the guard rail to see two of Crimilicious' punks from Proton making their way up the stairs. They were dressed very casually and already had their pistols—complete with silencers—at the ready. They gabbed innocuously to one another about their girlfriends. John could only hear them, but he couldn't make out their actual words. Nor did he have time to as they were closing the distance between he and themselves in a hurry.

John turned and headed back out into the hallway. As the door slowly closed on its own behind him, he swiveled each direction to decide which way to go. One direction had an elevator at the end of the hall and that's the direction he took. John ran down the hallway as fast as he could and began to frantically hit the side button. Fortunately for him, the elevator had already been at the second floor, so it opened almost immediately. The collector zipped into the elevator and hit the button to the fifth and top floor.

The door to the stairwell swung open and the Proton thugs entered the hallway and began to look around. They just happened to see the doors of the elevator close on John. The two killers ran over to the elevator and saw that it was headed for the fifth floor.

"Top floor!" one of the killers observed. "Come on." The two ran toward the stairwell once more.

Inside the elevator, John desperately looked around the elevator for some manner to evade his killers. The Proton thugs were straining with each step to beat the elevator to the top floor. John finally stopped looking around, because he saw exactly what the doctor ordered. *"Thank God this piece of crap wasn't updated to the 21st century,"* he thought.

The Proton killers entered the hallway to the fifth floor, breathing heavily. Looking around, they quickly found the elevator doorway. They ran over just in time for the elevator to ding and then automatically push open its doors. The killers had their pistols at the ready.

Inside was nothing.

"Where the fuck'd he go?!" one of the killers questioned aloud.

"He couldn't have disappeared," the other observed.

The two stepped into the elevator itself. One of them spied John's hat lying upside down in the corner.

"There's his hat..." one of the killers pointed out.

While they were distracted by the hat and general confusion, two gunshots rang out, hitting one killer in front of the head and the other in the side of the head. With barely a groan, they toppled to the floor in lifeless heaps.

John Fetaccini swung down from the hatch in the ceiling of the elevator and as soon as he hit the ground, kicked each of the bodies to make sure they were dead. After no movement was forthcoming from the corpses, John stuck his .38 Special into the pocket of his coat, then bent over and picked up his hat. He dusted it off slightly before placing it onto his head.

"First," John growled disdainfully before stepping back out of the elevator. He looked down both sides of the hallway to see if anyone else was coming. He turned and quickly walked towards the stairwell entrance, his head looking around to make sure he didn't miss anyone.

Back in room 214, Clemens was busy untying Juan Ortega from the chair he was bound to. The door swung open, much to Sarrageno's surprise and John entered.

"Leave his ass!" John frantically ordered. "Come on! We gotta go. NOW."

Clemens kicked over Ortega's chair, knocking him to the floor with a groan before following Sarrageno after

John, who had already left them behind. Ortega tried ineffectively to get out of the ropes he was still in.

"Little help?" he called out to no one in particular.

As John charged down the hotel's first floor hallway, Sarrageno and Clemens struggled to catch up.

"Geno, we got a phone around I can use?" John queried, presuming his men were still behind him.

"Sure," Sarrageno answered. "There's a pay phone out in the parking lot. I've got a slug you can use."

"What's the rush, John?" Clemens asked. "What's goin' on?"

"I'll tell ya later," John replied. "Let's just get outta here. And keep your eyes *open*."

John continued to move ahead as Sarrageno and Clemens briefly stopped to shrug at one another before following along.

At Crimilicious' living room over in Proton, he and his two associates were still lounging about the place watching television. Marijuana smoke hung over the room like a thick fog. A nearby cordless landline phone began to ring, jarring the three from their buzz.

"Man, shut that phone up!" Ty angrily commanded to no one in particular.

Jerome reached over and answered the phone. "What is it?" he curtly asked. "Who is this?"

It was John on the other end back in Puptown, on the pay phone outside the Crescent Moon Hotel. Sarrageno and Clemens chatted to one another behind him, but kept a good watch on what was going on around them.

"It's John Fetaccini," the new boss introduced himself. "Lemme speak to Sean."

"You mean Crimilicious, foo?" Jerome inquired as if someone got his order wrong.

"Whatever," John dismissed him. "Just put him on."

"Hold on," Jerome retorted impatiently. "Crim, it's John Fetaccini. You wanna talk to him?"

Crimilicious' head turned to face his pal. "Fetaccini?" he repeated for clarification. "Ain't he s'posed ta be dead?"

"Yeah..." Ty agreed. "S'posed ta be."

Crimilicious thought a bit, his mind cutting its way through the weed-induced haze as best it could. "Okay, give it here," he finally said. Jerome handed over the receiver to his boss.

"Whassup, man?" Crimilicious cheerfully greeted.

"Hello?" John asked as if someone had spoke Chinese to him.

"How'd you get dis numba?" Crimilicious questioned.

"Never mind how I got this number," John shot back. "Is this Crimilicious?"

"Himself," the Prince of Proton clarified. "Good to hear from ya. Sorry 'bout yer boss. He was a good guy. How's things now that you're in charge, man?"

"Bad news travels fast," John observed. "Not so well. Not well at all. You heard 'bout what happened to my old boss?" he asked with a skeptical squint. "Well, the same thing that happened to him almost happened to me."

"Yeah? So?" Crimilicious queried rhetorically. "Whaddaya want me ta do about it?"

"Oh, like you don't know anything about it?" John pressed.

"I don't know shit, man," Crimilicious answered, losing patience. "Whatchu doin' call me up at my house an' start tellin' me whut's whut?"

"Come on, Sean," John retorted. "I know you had somethin' to do with this just like you had somethin' to do with Cicci too. By the way, where is that piece a' shit Dimi? Is he there with you?"

"John, I think there's some kinda miscommunication," Crimilicious explained. "I don't know anything about what happened to Cicci."

"'Miscommunication'?!" John repeated. "Well, lemme make sure you hear this loud and clear: if you ever make a move on me again, I'm gonna gouge your eyes out and use your skull to hold my pencils. I'm gonna throw your fucking body in a cage with a wolverine on angel dust. I'm gonna—"

Crimilicious pulled his head away from the receiver derisively. "Hey, Fetaccini..." he interrupted.

"What?" John took the bait.

"Suck me dry," Crimilicious spat out before hanging up the phone.

"You motherfucker!" John bellowed as he slammed his receiver against the base of the phone. "Get the fuck back on here you cocksucking piece a' shit!!" Moments later, John managed to break the end of the receiver before Sarrageno and Clemens pulled him away in an attempt to calm him down.

"Calm down, John!" Sarrageno suggested.

"Yeah, he's gone," Clemens added. "Let's go!"

"This is bullshit, man!" John decreed.

Clemens and Sarrageno succeeded in pulling John far enough away that he just decided to walk away with them. Clemens was damned glad he didn't offer to let John use his cell phone.

Outside the kitchen of the Fountainstone Lodge, Cora was propped up against a brick wall in an alley with another female Italian employee, who smoked a cigarette while they were on a break. Her employee friend had good looks that had visibly been damaged by smoking that made her look older than she really was. Long, stringy, brown hair hung down either side of her head and into her face.

"Aren't you supposed to be in the marathon next weekend?" Cora asked, all but gesturing to her friend's cigarette.

"Yeah, so?" the employee shot back, taking the cigarette from her mouth to speak.

"You really think that's a good idea?" Cora asked, legitimately concerned.

"Think what's a good idea?" her friend replied as she blew smoke from her mouth.

John rushed in next to them, grabbing Cora's attention away.

"Hey, John!" Cora cheerfully greeted. "What's going on? You look sick."

"It's nothing," John waved her off. "Cora, I hate to ask you this, but I need your help big time. Can you get off and come with me?"

"Uh... I dunno," Cora stated uncertainly. She turned to her friend, still smoking like a furnace. "Can you cover for me?"

"Pfft, hell no," the other employee scoffed. "Afternoon rush is about ta come in. You know how crazy it gets."

Cora turned back to her man to deliver the bad news. "Sorry, John," she began. "I'm workin' here."

Whatever John's plan involving Cora was, he couldn't come up with an alternative. He eventually muttered a "Yeah, alright."

"I'll see you tonight?" Cora asked apologetically.

"Sure," the collector responded half-heartedly.

The other employee took a drag as she noticed John for the first time. "Hey, didn't I give you some money for Jerry's Kids?"

"Uh, no, that was my brother," John lied through his teeth before turning and wandering off all alone. Cora and her friend headed back into the lodge.

"Coulda sworn I saw that guy before," the employee thought aloud as she tossed her still-lit cigarette over her shoulder.

John went back home and made a beeline for his bedroom. He plopped down in the wooden rocking chair, not even bothering to take his coat or hat off. He looked pensive and brooding and was in desperate need of decompression. This was the first time anyone had actually tried to kill him and the idea of it had finally caught up with him. Every so often, his feet would fidget with the floor.

At one point, he even fell asleep in the chair and was still there, sitting in the dark when Cora came home that evening. John heard her slight tromping sounds in the distance, but his reaction was negligible. The bedroom door swung open and the light came on, revealing the entire room, Cora in the doorway, and John in the rocking chair. Cora was still dressed in her lodge uniform. John slowly turned his head to look at her.

"Hey," Cora said.

"Hey," John answered.

"You upset cause I couldn't get off work?" she inquired.

"Nah," John lied. "Not really."

Cora sat her purse onto the dresser, then knelt and sat down on the floor in front of John. He gave her a slight smile.

"I didn't know you had a brother, John," she began.

"I don't," he stated. Cora decided not to press it. Instead she just looked at him, hoping he would share whatever was obviously on his mind.

"I don't think I can do it, Cora," John finally spoke up. "I don't think I wanna do it."

"Do what, John?" Cora asked for clarification.

"Be in charge," the new boss answered.

"What's wrong, John?" his woman inquired. "Isn't this what you wanted? Something new?"

John sat there just looking at Cora as he rocked in the chair. He then bent his head down to look at nothing in particular.

"I had to kill two people today, Cora..." John finally admitted. Cora's stomach bubbled up like a bad case of heartburn. There was an uncomfortable silence the seemed to last 10 minutes, but was probably only 20 seconds.

"I've never killed anyone before," John eventually said. "I collect money. I don't make people go place bets and I certainly don't make them welch on 'em. Sure, I beat the hell out of people when they won't be reasonable or if they need to do the right thing and won't. I'm just doing a job as a consequence of their actions, not mine."

Cora looked blankly at the floor, but she listened to every word John said. "What happened?" she questioned lowly.

"We were trying get some information out of this mook about who killed Cicci," John continued. "Yes, we knocked him around some cause he was tryin' to hold out on us. He was, by the way. But we didn't kill him. I'm heading off to the stairwell cause there's less people that use them when the elevators are right there and let's face it, I could use the exercise. So I go into the stairwell and I see two of Crimilicious' punks coming up."

"Who is that?" Cora asked.

"He's in charge of the black gang over in Proton," John said in an off-handed manner. "Anyway, they got guns... and silencers. I know how this story ends. So I ran out of the stairwell and into the elevator and climbed up into the-the hatch, I guess?"

"They still have those?" Cora queried. "I haven't seen one a' those in a long time."

"This one did," John continued, "else, I wouldn't be here now. So I get up in the hatch John McClane-style and when the elevator opens there they are. They get into the elevator, they can't find me, and I shot 'em. Both in the head." He gestured the gunshot to his head for punctuation. "I've done plenty of bad things but I never had to break the ol' 'thou shall not kill' commandment."

"Well..." Cora began, fidgeting her legs on the floor before looking up at John. "It does say 'thou shall not kill' but not 'thou shall just stand there and let thou kill... thee?' Did you do something? Do you know why this... other guy wanted to kill you?"

"I have no fuckin' clue, Cora," John responded. "Gang shit, probably. They don't like ya, so they just pop ya," he again gestured a gunshot to the head. "We found out Cicci's driver Dimi set him up, though."

"Dimi?" Cora asked at no one in particular. "Is that that little weasely guy that's always leering at my chest?"

"That's him," John said.

"Figures. That guy's a douchenozzle," Cora scoffed. She looked away again momentarily, before turning back to face John and lean in on the arm rest of the rocking chair. "This killing business isn't..." she began, "...isn't good, John. I'm sick just thinking of it."

"Me too," John admitted.

"But," Cora continued, "I don't... think... I don't think badly of you. It's self-defense. Like you told me, it's not good to have to hit people, but it is good to defend yourself. And really, that's all you've done: defend yourself. It's the most extreme instance you've ever dealt with, but that's all it is. I'd rather those people not be dead now, but if it's them or you, then *them*! Fuck those guys and their boss *and* his goofy-ass name!"

John sat there looking at Cora momentarily speechless before breaking into a fit of laughter. Cora smiled and involuntarily followed suit.

"Fuck those guys and their boss and his goofy-ass name," John repeated. There was another pause.

"So you want it back the way it was?" Cora broke the silence.

"It can't be the way it was," John said dourly.

"Why not?" Cora pressed.

"Cicci's dead," John explained.

"That's true," Cora agreed. "But... there's still some good that could come out of this."

"What're you talkin' about?" John asked.

"If Cicci made you the boss, you'd do it no questions, right?" Cora answered a question with a question.

"Yeah," John replied.

"But he didn't do that," Cora explained. "He died before he could do that. You don't owe those guys anything. You do what you think is right and don't let any of 'em bully you into anything different. You really think they're gonna say or do anything against you? You're John Fetaccini, dammit. They know better than to mess with you. Everyone knows that when you have to ask questions, they come wrapped in knuckle sandwiches."

John smiled. Cora raised up to her knees and gave him a kiss on the side of the face.

"Feel better?" Cora asked.

"Ehhh..." John shook his flat palm. "It's not you. Cicci's funeral's tomorrow. I need to think of somethin'. Everyone's gonna be there. You know, Cicci was like a second dad after my first one left. He saw me in the street one day and took me in for no real reason."

"Maybe he had a feeling about you," Cora interjected, "like I did."

"Maybe," John shrugged. "Who knows? I'm gonna miss him a lot."

"Wa—what," Cora stammered. "What do you want, John?"

"I want..." John turned to look at Cora's face. "I want to wake up every morning. To know you're gonna be there. Or I'm gonna be there. That's all."

"Okay," Cora said understandingly before standing up to her feet. "Come on, let's go out ta eat. You've had a rough day."

"Okay, but you pick," John retorted as he stood up out of the chair. "I've thought enough today."

"Fine..." Cora good-naturedly said. She put her arm around John and led him to the bedroom's door and into the hallway. "Hey John..." she began. "What do you call a fish with no eyes?"

John thought about it a second, but nothing came to him. "I dunno," he gave up. "What?"

"Fsh," Cora hissed as an answer. It elicited a chuckle out of them both.

"That's pretty good, Cora," John said in all sincerity.

"No, it's not," Cora admitted.

Later that night after an especially delicious meal at Taco Bell filled with tacos and quesadillas, John and Cora managed to return to their apartment minutes before an immense rainstorm moved over Klaude and the Puptown area in particular. The electricity went off once briefly, but returned just as quickly as it had left.

Cora snoozed happily in their bed while John—unable to sleep—stood at the window, watching the storm. Apparently, he had not thought enough for the day as all he could do is wonder what he was going to do the next day. There were no plans forthcoming and as a result, neither was any sleep. John would have to accept watching the flying water harmlessly hit and drain down the glass window as a consolation prize.

Every so often, he would turn back to watch Cora sleeping, but then go back to the storm as if there were answers to be had somewhere out there.

CHAPTER 11 - Ostentatious Display

The next day at Rizzo's Funeral Parlor, limos and ritzy-looking cars were lined up along the street. Inside the chapel, Cicci's funeral was beginning. Cicci lay in an open casket dressed in a deep blue dead-man's suit. He looked more like an artist's recreation of Cicci instead of the real thing. Flowers were virtually everywhere. Massive, monstrous displays of floral arrangements encrusted the walls. A piteous organ requiem played in the distance.

The pews were nearly filled to capacity. It was mostly Italians, including John's work associates. There were weeping women and forlorn men. Sniffling and coughing echoed louder than usual in the church. Even Crimilicious and his crew showed up and even though they were dressed in their Sunday church finery, they were really just playing lip-service. Ty especially wanted to be gone.

Suddenly, John Fetaccini entered from the rear. He was wearing his normal street clothes except his hat. He turned and slammed the doors shut behind himself, causing those gathered to gasp and whirl around to see him. Some murmured amongst themselves about what was happening.

"What the hell is John doing?" Clemens hissed to his pals.

"He know this is a funeral?" Sarrageno shrugged.

"Maybe he's drunk," Sabelli suggested.

"Look at dat foo," Ty grumbled.

Crimilicious kept an eye on John, unimpressed with his showboating shenanigans. John, meanwhile, marched straight up to Cicci's casket. He leaned over and studied the corpse.

"Cicci... how ya doin'?" John asked as if he were actually lying there. "You've looked better."

"What's he sayin'?" Vinelli inquired.

"Does he know how big of an ass he's being?" Robert asked rhetorically.

"Shh!" De Luna countered.

"I know it's not what you probably wanted," John continued. "But I gotta step down, Cicci. I can't be the boss no more. I don't know how you did it so long." John turned slightly to his friends. "You need someone to collect money an' run errands," he began, "come find me. You need some dirtbag that likes ta run things, go get Donald Trump. Otherwise, I'm out."

"Come on, John. Don't do this," Clemens spoke up from his pew.

"You happy for this show they're puttin' on for ya, Cicci?" John asked, ignoring his pal's objections. "I hope it's amusin' ya..." He paused. "Course it's not. It ain't amusin' me either."

John slowly pulled out his .38 Special and opened fire on the floral arrangements, blasting them to shreds. The gathered mostly shrieked or ducked beneath the pews or some combination of both. John's work associates just sat there in a stupor, unsure what to make of this madness. Crimilicious and his crew were stone-faced.

"What's wrong with you?!" Gagi demanded to know.

"John, what the hell are you doin'?!" Sarrageno rebuked.

John kept shooting up the various floral arrangements. The mourners had had enough and suddenly jumped to their feet in outrage.

"Fetaccini, you brain damaged or somethin'?!" Crimilicious shouted. "You can't do this shit in no funeral, man!"

John reloaded his pistol, spun the cylinder before clamping it shut, then slowly turned around. He marched right up to Crimilicious and jammed his pistol into the punk's forehead. No one was sure what would happen next and everyone was afraid to even move. Even Crimilicious' crew weren't going for their guns out of fear of John pulling the trigger.

Crimilicious stood there callously unflinching with John's pistol between his eyes. Ever so slowly, John's finger made to squeeze the trigger... and then relaxed. He emptied the pistol's cylinder, catching the six bullets in his left hand. Crimilicious wasn't sure what to make of this. He'd never show someone else this kind of mercy... but he wasn't about to let John know how relieved he was.

"If a hair on Cora's head is split," John began in a growling cadence. "If I see any a' your boys in Puptown... If I even *feel* like you or someone you know are creepin' around me, you die just like that," he snapped his fingers for effect. "But for today... you live."

John turned and trudged off for the rear of the chapel. Once he got there, he swung open the doors and exited, leaving the funeral and its mourners behind.

Outside the parlor, Cora stood there, dressed up in a nice red dress with a thin, brown wool coat over it. She was carrying a picnic basket and holding John's hat. The door of the parlor opened and John emerged. He made a beeline straight for her.

"Is it done?" Cora inquired.

"It's done," John replied.

"Good," Cora stated. "You'll feel a lot better once things get back to normal and when you get some food in your stomach." She held up the basket for emphasis.

John and Cora turned and started down the sidewalk when suddenly, the funeral parlor's doors swung open and out stepped Crimilicious and his crew. Ty and Jerome were incensed.

"Yo, Fetaccini!" Crimilicious barked.

John turned around and noticing who it was, he involuntarily pushed Cora behind himself and held out his arm in an instinctive manner to protect her.

Jerome started to pull out his piece, but Crimilicious took notice and slapped it out of his hands.

"Put that shit away!" the Prince of Proton commanded. "Ain't done nuthin' ta you! I ain't playin' now!"

Like a mewling child, Jerome scuttled away for his gun and pocketed it.

"Fetaccini..." Crimilicious began. The two looked at each other for an uncomfortably long amount of time like they were about to gun each other down to Ennio Morricone music. "Respec," the crime boss finally said.

John did a jaunty half-salute before turning away to leave with Cora. As they walked, she wrapped her fingers around his. She then put on John's hat and looked at him with a grin.

"It looks nicer on you," John said, not really lying but not really buying it either. "Everything looks better on you," he added.

It was well after 9:00 p.m. as John and Cora walked on a sidewalk, still carrying the picnic basket but now also a blanket. Cora's head was draped on John's shoulder and he had his free arm around her.

"I was watching this movie that was taped off TV in like '88 or some shit," Cora said.

"Mm-hmm?" John grunted.

"The movie went 25 minutes before the first commercial break," Cora informed.

"Whoa... !" John replied like he'd just entered the Matrix.

"Damned right, whoa," Cora agreed. "And that's not all. The commercial break was two minutes long and included only *four* commercials!"

"God, I miss the way they did things in the 80s," John sighed. "So, did you have a good day today?"

"Pretty okay day today, it being a half-day an' all," Cora replied. "Somebody brought their kid in and he vomited mashed corn all over the carpet. I wasn't about to clean that shit up, so I went on break."

John laughed. Cora merely grinned.

"Say Cora..." John spoke up. "You remember the first time we met?"

"Oh, man..." Cora replied unenthusiastically. "That has to be the most embarrassing how-we-met story ever."

"Ain't nothin' embarassin' about it," John protested.

"What have you, gone tilt? We were in jail!" Cora exclaimed.

"So?" John dismissively said. "You were in your rebellious stage and tried to swipe that television."

"If you have a better way to celebrate a Lakers' victory, I'd like to hear it," Cora defensively justified. "Besides, what were *you* doin' there? Spray paintin' a building wasn't it? Caught a bad case of slow that day?"

"Hey, that ain't the point," John explained. "The point is when I first saw you being pushed in while they were pushin' me out, I thought 'There goes the best-lookin' girl in Klaude'."

"You're kidding, right?" Cora incredulously asked.

"Oh, I said it," John affirmed. "Ask Clemens. Good thing I saved that Monopoly chance card to get me outta jail. I also remember how pissed your mom was when I asked you out."

"Man, she hated you, didn't she?" Cora remembered.

"Eh, some people are jus' haters for no reason I guess," John surmised.

"I sure am glad I didn't listen to Mom about you," Cora revealed.

"Yeah?"

"Yeah."

"That's nice. Thanks a lot," John said, bending down to kiss Cora on the top of her head. Cora looked skyward.

"Hey John?" she said with a smile.

"Yeah?" he answered.

"You know what I'd like more than anything?" Cora asked.

"I can't imagine..." John replied. Except he could, or it was more he could imagine what he wanted her to do.

Cora stopped and looked right into John's face. "A piggy-back ride."

"Hop on, baby," John said without a second thought. He bent down so Cora could climb onto his back. He rose up, carrying her as they moved down the sidewalk, the basket swinging in Cora's hand. She almost looked like a little girl.

"This is nice," Cora cooed.

The sky's twinkling stars could easily be seen from the hilltop overlooking the city's lake. John and Cora sat on the blanket together, chewing on goodies with their basket sitting nearby.

"...and that's why the French don't wash," John said, finishing an explanation we were just not privy to. Cora laughed heartily.

"It's so beautiful here…" Cora observed. "No wonder you like it. This would be a great spot to get married."

"This would be a great spot for the end of a good date," John added.

Cora lightly punched John in the arm and chuckled.

"I don't do that in public," she stated.

"Yet," John qualified.

"Yeah, keep dreamin'," Cora retorted.

"Hey Cora," John spoke up, changing the subject. "Didja hear about the guy that lost his left arm and leg in a car crash?"

"No, that sounds awful!" Cora said with concern. "What happened?"

"He's *all right* now," John said with a grin and looked at Cora with a self-assured expression.

"How do you come up with such silly things to say?" Cora asked with a chuckle.

"I have a pair of writers living in my footlocker," John said, hitching his thumb behind him to nothing in particular.

As her giggle came to an end, Cora rested her head on John's shoulder. "Hey, John?" she asked.

"Yes, sweetheart?" the collector answered.

There was an odd silence, but then suddenly Cora spoke up. "BRAINS!" she growled.

John actually shrieked, causing Cora to break out into another fit of laughter. She pulled his face to hers and made up for her little prank with a passionate kiss.

THE END

Lightning Source UK Ltd.
Milton Keynes UK
UKHW011010210820
368606UK00001B/219